Ride High Pineapple

Ride the highs and lows of life with 13-year-old skateboarding enthusiast, Issy, as she battles with facial difference, bullying, broken hearts, betrayal, and blossoming love. Ride High Pineapple is a compelling, insightfully written, uplifting story about overcoming your own fears, insecurities, and limitations.

— Jacqui Halpin, Author

A new voice on the contemporary middle-grade scene. A real story about being different and overcoming the challenges it brings.

— Raelene Purtill, Author, Stringybark Stories YA Short Story Winner 2012

Ride High Pineapple is a delightful middle-grade book. This well-written book kept me turning the pages as Issy learns to confront her worse fears with the help of her friends.

— Jeanette O'Hagan, Author, Blogger and Poet

Empowering story about Issy, a tormented teenage girl who defies the bullies, gaining her self-worth.

— Karen Tyrrell resilience Author

Ride High Pineapple is a raw, honest story filled with courage and hope.

— Dana Blackhall, Australian Crouzon and Pfeiffer Syndromes Support Group

Adolescence is a tough gig, but Issy Burgess has a few added challenges—facial difference, anxiety, *and* a relentless bully. Issy's story of confronting her fears and working through her difficulties will inspire middle grade readers. Kudos to Jenny Woolsey for writing *Ride High Pineapple*. It ticks all the boxes: skateboarding, besties, and boys. And it's chock-a-block full of hope, insight, and solid strategies for handling bullying and managing anxiety. A must for school libraries and school counsellors!

— Alison Stegert, School Counsellor & Kidlit Author

Ride High Pineapple is a book I couldn't put down once I started – and once I finished I couldn't forget it. This story is not just for those who have felt different, been bullied or for all those not in the 'in group' - it's for every teenager and every person who interacts with others. Jenny has written a book for everyone.

— Karen Haworth, RN & Diabetes Educator

Ride High Pineapple is not just for people born with Crouzon syndrome, it will resonate with anyone who is bullied for being different. Issy shows us all how to be an overcomer. Everyone can ride high like Issy.

— Kerry Tognella, International Crouzon Syndrome Support Group

Ride High
Pineapple

Jenny Woolsey

Pearls of Wisdom Press

To my beautiful daughter Melissa, *whose inner strength and courage are an inspiration to all.*

Contents

Foreword

Ride High Pineapple

I had the pleasure of reading *Ride High Pineapple* on a plane leaving Dallas, Texas, where I work as the Executive Director for Children's Craniofacial Association, a national nonprofit organization dedicated to helping empower children and families affected by facial differences. I know my seat neighbor was certainly curious as to what I was reading, since I couldn't hold back audible laughter at times. Other times, I sat in stunned silence remembering my own experiences as a child with a facial difference.

The book resonated with me in a special way … you see, I too was a teenage girl who felt mostly normal, except others did not always see me that way. Like Issy, I was shy and uncertain a lot of the time. I had friends, but I also had people who enjoyed making my life difficult. Sometimes, the stress of feeling awkward and alone was almost too great to bear, but I made it through with books and blogs, so that's why I'm so grateful for stories like this one.

Reading Jenny's words – for she too knows what it's like – helped me peek back into my own childhood through a different lens. Issy's story is one that many kids face and her subtle triumphs are a chorus of encouragement for kids with differences. I particularly like that Issy goes through the same emotional experiences as other kids, like jealousy, name-calling in anger, and the temptation to lie. Furthermore, Issy simultaneously wants to blend in *and* stand out. She is incredibly relatable and above all, a universal character. Though her specific struggle is having a facial difference, kids across the world know what it is like to be teased because of their looks. It does not feel good and we all have the power to step in, when we see someone being targeted. Issy's good friends in the story stand by her and I hope that is the message that all readers walk away with: individually we may be vulnerable, but together we are strong. With love and support from our friends, we are able to advocate for ourselves and tell our own stories. We are able to stand confidently in front of our peers and bullies and assert our own self-worth. Books like *Ride High Pineapple* give our kids a platform to bring awareness to their classrooms and schools and reassurance that they are not alone.

I know you will enjoy this book immensely and please share it with your friends! Tell them that facial differences are just a part of our lives, and not the entirety of who we are. Tell them that differences come from syndromes – like Crouzon, Apert, and Treacher Collins – but also come from injuries, accidents, and genetic differences. Tell them not to be afraid to be friends with someone who looks different! It is always possible to be kind. Finally, direct your friends to our website, www.ccakids.org, to learn about more kids like Issy and find out how you can join the movement to make the world a kinder place.

Erica Mossholder
Executive Director

children's craniofacial association

www.ccakids.org

Chapter One

Monday, 2 March

7:04 a.m.

Secrets. You know; those things you don't tell your parents, brothers or sisters. If they are super secrets, you don't even tell them to your best friend. You don't tell *anyone*. All teenagers have them, and if they say they don't, they're lying. Secrets can be about all kinds of things. There's no set rules or guidelines for what they are.

Today is the day I'm actually going to reveal one of mine. Now I guess you could classify it as a semi-secret or a half secret, as some people already know it. My family, best friend and primary school classmates do. This secret is something very important about *me*. It has made me who I am; well the outside of me anyway.

In five hours' time, in English, I will be setting my secret loose like a paper plane on the wind, to my Year Nine classmates. I'm not normally one to tell my personal secrets to my class, but I have a major problem at school, that I haven't been able to solve. We've been given this assignment which I'm presenting today, and I'm praying the idea I've come up with, will stop what's happening.

Let me tell you about my problem. It isn't an academic problem, or a money problem, or a friendship problem. It's a *she* problem. Actually to expand on that, *she's* a nasty, beastly girl problem. *Her* name – TIA. (I hate writing her name in my journal, so I call her *The Beast*.) Last August, in Year Eight, The Beast was plonked into my class. The rumour going around was that she was expelled from Bishop Park High, in the next town, because she threatened a girl with a knife. The Beast knew absolutely nothing about me but I was her instant target. She didn't even start with, 'What's your name?' or 'Hi, my name's Tia,' or 'What's wrong with your eyes?' It was instantly, 'Hey you, Fish Face!' This shocked me so much, I didn't know what to do.

I've been called names in school before for how my eyes look, but the last time was in primary school and didn't last very long. A kid called Tyrone Bell liked to call me, 'Poppy Eyes'. My eight-year-old reaction back then

16

was to stick my hand up in front of his face and say, 'Stop it. I don't like it!' which we had been taught to do. After a couple of weeks, he got sick and tired of me shoving my hand at his eyeballs, and he gave up.

This problem with The Beast has been going on for way, way longer than two weeks.

For the first nine years of my life, stares and being pointed at happened regularly. Not so much at kindy or school (except for Tyrone), but out and about where I wasn't known, like at the playground or the shops. I'd hear snickers, comments and whispers from both adults and children. Mum would try and protect me from them but I knew what was happening. I knew I was different and I couldn't do anything about it.

At the age of nine I had a major operation which made my face and eyes look more normal. (I won't go into details.) That was good as the teasing and stares all stopped. The problem though is that your face grows and changes. It morphs from your child face to your adult face... so my face has been changing too – but it's going back to what it was like before my operation – that means my eyes are big again. Not as big as they were when I was little, but still big enough to be different to everyone else's.

The Beast has taken it upon herself to remind me of this fact on a daily basis. The first time she hit me with her cruel words, last year, my lame reaction was to burst into tears. That toddler-like behaviour delighted her, and she laughed hysterically at me, sounding exactly like that green-faced Wicked Witch of the West in the *Wizard of Oz*.

The teasing freaked me out so much that I tried to avoid her. I'd walk around the class the opposite direction to her, and sit as far away from her as I could. If she was at the back, I'd be at the front. If she was on the left side, I'd be on the right. Going from class to class, I'd ensure she'd be metres away from me. Despite all my concerted efforts, it still happened. When she did call me 'Fish Face' or 'Googly Eyes' or 'Popcorn' or whatever else she felt like, I'd do the 'ignore her' thing, outwardly silent but inwardly a flaming bucking bull. I hoped she'd give up because I wasn't reacting... but she kept on going. If you opened up my chest and looked at my heart, you'd see a giant stab wound caused by The Beast's viciousness.

Tilly, my best friend, knows a bit about what's going on, but not everything, as I haven't told her. I know I should tell her but I don't want her interfering and making matters worse. Tilly is an awesome best friend, and we've been friends since Year Two, but she can get carried away with being my protector. I don't want her making a scene, like, what if Tilly tells The Beast off and then I'm threatened with a knife? ☹ That would be mind-blowingly horrible!

Before school started this year, I prayed like crazy (yes I believe in God), that The Beast would be in a different Form class, but she's with me again. Ugh! Every morning this term, she's greeted me cordially with her ugly names, and whenever she's wanted something, it's, 'Hey Fish Face, can I have a sharpener?' or 'Hey Popcorn, can I borrow your eraser?' Like that's my name. And how do I react? The same as last year. I can't even say, 'Stop it. I don't like it!' or even, 'My name is Issy.' or 'Get lost Tia!' or 'No you can't have my pen.' Though I don't think that would stop her anyway. She's such a skunk. ☹

Around midday, it'll all be over. My secret about my face will be no more. I'll let you know this afternoon how it goes. Will The Beast stop her bullying?

Chapter Two

4:01 p.m.

Yay, I did it – I presented my speech! ☺ I was *so* nervous. On the scale of 1 to 10, ten being the worst, I was a 10. You see, I also suffer from nerves. Mum calls it *anxiety*. When my anxiety is severe, like a 10 or even a 12 (off the scale), I get really stressed out. More than other people do when they get nervous. For me, my brain goes all crazy and heaps of thoughts pound around in circles, like race horses galloping around the track on Melbourne Cup Day. Today's were; *What if I forget my speech? What if I get laughed at? What if all my classmates start calling me names? What will The Beast do?* My body goes all wild too. I get the trembles, the sweats and my heart beats like a bongo drum. I'm basically a bit of a basket case. When I'm like this, I usually chicken out and don't do whatever it is. Once I tried to keep going but I threw up which was hugely humiliating.

Now, that's when my anxiety is really bad. It's not always like that thank goodness. Sometimes if the situation is just a little stressful, a 5 or 6 on the scale, I'll get one or two of the symptoms (sweats, pounding heart). I felt this way last year when I had to present a poem to the class. At these times I can push ahead with what I have to do. (I recited my poem and got a B.) It's when my brain decides to have its hissy fit that I have problems – it's hard to tame my brain. ☹

Let me tell you what happened:

At twelve-fifteen the revelation of my secret began with my teacher, Miss O'Keefe, calling me, 'Your turn Issy.' (She was smiling because she likes me. ☺)

My feet shuffled up to the whiteboard. It wasn't that far but it felt like from here to the sun away. I turned, took a deep breath and put my prepared plan into action. I thought this plan might help keep my anxiety at bay – I'd read it in a girl's blog on the Internet. The plan being that I would imagine that my classmates were wooden zombies. I moved my eyes to the back wall above them where there was a laminated poster of Shakespeare.

What a weird looking dude with that fancy frill around his neck. Why'd he wear those clothes? I thought.

I stared at him, procrastinating. At this point I felt like a 7.

Miss coughed. She didn't have a cold so that meant I *had* to start... I opened my mouth to speak and the anxiety hit me like a sledgehammer. My heart beat so fast I thought it might mountain-climb out of my chest and up my throat. Sweat beads bubbled on my forehead. I wiped them with a tissue. Then my brain started. I had hit 10 on the Richter scale.

Is telling my secret a good thing to be doing? It'll probably backfire on me. Maybe I should leave that part out... But Miss knows I'm going to say it...

I knew I could leave my secret out quite easily. I'd written ten billion drafts of the speech (well you know what I mean) and I'd rehearsed it every night sitting at my dressing table. I knew every pink, oil-filled pimple and sun freckle on my face. My tummy began to do flip-flops.

Am I going to be sick again?

I swallowed and looked at Miss for support.

'Okay Issy, it's time to start,' Miss said in a soft voice. She smiled at me with encouragement. I would have to decide quickly when I got up to that part of my speech. My heart pounded.

Can I run out of the room and not do it at all?

'You can do it Issy,' Miss said.

I began...

'Good morning Miss O'Keefe and 9.04. I'm Isabella Marie Burgess. I was born on the 8th of July, at St Peter's Private Hospital. I have a mum and a dad and a little brother, Nathan. I also have a pet Maltese puppy called Snowy and three hermit crabs called Zackman, Cavey and Rockmiester. I love skateboarding, drawing and writing poetry. I own two skateboards and one ripstick. This is my penny board.'

I held up my purple board with its red wheels, which had coloured photos of me, my family and pets tacked all over it. (I chose the ones where I looked the prettiest.)

'I have been boarding for two years. I feel free when I'm riding with the wind on my face. I can do some tricks and I'm learning more. I'll now demonstrate to you a kickflip.'

I managed to execute my kickflip in the tiny space. It wasn't easy as the desks were close. Some of the photos spiralled to the floor and a couple of others became scrunched. I left the photos where they landed and picked up my sketchpad. I was now back to a 6.

'I like to sketch Anime characters. It's fun. I use drawing pencils and water colour pencils. Here's a picture of Arisa I drew the other day.'

I moved around the class. Kids glanced at the drawing and Rachel said, 'That's good.' I continued back to the front.

'I like to write poetry, especially poetry that rhymes, like this one:

The sky is blue, the flowers sway
The breeze is warm, this summer day.
Waves are lapping, sand is warm
The clouds grow black, it's gonna storm!'

Then my legs began to shake. If I had a bit of rope I would've tied them together. I gazed at Shakespeare again. I zoomed back up to a 9.

Hey Shakespeare, climb out of that picture and cometh down here. Thou canst deliver the next part for me!

This was it. I had to make a quick decision. I'd look stupid if I just stood there. Talking to Shakespeare wouldn't solve my problem. I sucked the musty air down into my lungs. It was time to either keep, or release, my secret. My hands shook, more sweat bubbled, and my heart thumped.

Keep going, a voice in my head said.

'I was born with a condition called Crouzon syndrome. The affected gene in my DNA made the bones in my skull and face stop growing too soon. People with this syndrome have misshapen heads, big eyes due to their small eye sockets, and flat faces. I've had twelve surgeries so far, for a variety of things, and I will have more when I get older. The photos on the skateboard I showed you are from all the parts of my life. Since I was little, people have pointed at me and said mean things about my eyes. I wish they'd stop. I know my eyes are big. I know I'm different and I can't do anything about it. I can't hide my face so I've had to accept what is.'

There it was, I had revealed my secret and my feelings. It was flying around the classroom on its invisible paper plane. Would it land in The Beast's heart? I sucked in more air. Now I needed to finish and sit down. In the back of my mind the worry was beginning to spin like a whirlpool.

'In conclusion, I'm Issy and I just happen to have Crouzons. It's a part of me but it doesn't define me. I love skateboarding, drawing and writing poetry. Peace!' I gave the peace sign.

I exhaled. It was done. Over. I twisted towards the teacher's desk. Miss was beaming and her eyes were twinkling. All right, now I waited for how they, my class, and in particular, The Beast, were going to react. I should've been pumped that I'd worked through my anxiety, that I hadn't run off or thrown up, but I wasn't. I looked at the floor, bracing myself for something insulting from The Beast or even the jerk boys who sat in the back, trying to look tough. They'd already made rude comments about Zac who went before me. He liked dance. But all I could hear was the teacher next door yelling at his class. Silence reigned in 9.04's English classroom. Just silence.

'*Isabella thou shouldst sit down now.*' I could hear Shakespeare drawing me like a magnet back to my seat.

I took some steps, studying the bits of grey fluff stuck to the carpet. A single clap, like a crack of thunder, shattered the room. A crescendo of clapping followed. I yanked my head up and stared at my classmates, scanning from row to row, side to side. They were *all* clapping. Even The Beast and the jerks. I was stoked! I plopped down on my chair and put my head in my hands.

Was I worried about nothing? Have I solved The Beast problem?

Do you think I have?

Chapter Three

5:09 p.m.

After the speeches, the rest of English flashed by. My brain did continual replay loops of my talk and the class's reaction, as the teacher's voice droned on, as background white noise.

'Well done Issy! I knew you could do it,' Miss O'Keefe said to me as I floated out of the room.

I smiled at her. 'Thanks Miss.' I didn't dare tell her that I had no clue what she had taught after the speeches.

Our next subject was Science. I strolled across the quadrangle to the lab, enjoying my newfound happiness, oblivious to the world around me.

'Hey Isabella!' I heard my name and instinctively turned my head to see who the voice belonged to, though the instant knot-in-my-belly suspicion told me who.

It was her. The Beast. It hadn't taken long, had it? Was I only getting one minute of bliss? I stared at her, sussing her out. Her face had its regular expression. She used my name. She sounded polite.

Is she going to apologise or say something nice? Is this the moment I've been waiting for? Will this be the end of my bullying?

She jogged to join me, her ponytail swishing. My heart thumped.

'Good talk, Googly Eyes.'

What? OMG. She hasn't changed at all!

I glared into her ugly face which had instantly morphed into a smug look. I felt my face redden as I gasped. She grinned. She knew she had totally hit the mark. I spun and power walked the last few metres to the lab. Her cackles echoed in my ears. That stab wound in my heart widened. It would soon be the San Andreas Fault Line.

Outside the room I stood with the others. It was horrible. There was no point telling anyone. I didn't want to be seen as a dobber.

Hurry up Sir. I want to go in.

I kept my head down, and studied the divots in the concrete.

Another voice, a young male's, invaded my thoughts. 'Issy I didn't know you could board. How long have you been doing that for?'

My heart jumped. *Is that—?*

I spun in the direction of the question, in anticipation. I couldn't believe it.

OMG it was who I thought - Tim Matheson. He was the cutest boy in my class and I had the biggest crush on him.

☺ My heart jumped like it was skipping Double Dutch. I loved Tim's squeezable dimples; his greenish-blue eyes, with flecks of gold in them; his soft, curly, shoulder-length, light brown hair; and his humour – he was just so funny. He wasn't class clown funny. I would call him storytelling, jokester funny. ☺ Tim has never really talked to me, except for maybe an occasional, 'Hi', so at that moment I suddenly felt all flustered.

While my heart cartwheeled, I tried to act all casual, telling him, 'I got my first board for Christmas two years ago.'

He nodded.

From behind him, The Beast glared at me. If she had arrows in her eyes, I would be the bullseye spot on a target.

'That kickflip was good,' he then said, smiling at me. His smile lit up his face like the bright sun on a summer's day.

My cheeks burnt. Maybe they were sun-kissed...lol ☺

'Thanks...' I replied. I really wanted to say more but my tongue felt like a heavy rock in my mouth and my legs felt like soft jelly snakes.

The Science lab door opened and the other kids bounded in while I slithered (well you know what I mean). Tia pushed past me, knocking me into a desk. Nobody else mentioned my not-a-secret-anymore-secret to me. I guessed that was a good thing, though a, 'Great trick' or 'Cool drawing' or 'Nice poem', or something like that, would've been nice.

At lunchtime, Tilly, (remember, she's my best friend) wanted to know how my talk had gone.

She said, 'How did your talk go?' ... lol

I told her, 'I *was so* nervous. I nearly ran off.' I bent my knees in a dramatic fashion. 'But I kept going and it went all right. I explained about my face – I nearly left it out though – *and* everyone clapped at the end.'

'Woohoo! You did it! You go girl,' she said, high fiving me. She's always been my cheer leader. A bit of chocolate spread landed on my finger. I licked it off – sharing – wasn't that what best friends did? 'Did anyone say anything about your face?'

I had to be honest.

'The Beast did on the way to Science. She called me Googly Eyes. I thought she was going to be nice. I should've known it wouldn't change her. Nobody else said anything.' I flicked off some fluff that was stuck to my navy shorts.

'The witch! You should tell on her. It's been going on for way too long. And if you don't, I will. She has no right to say stuff about your eyes.' Tilly's eyes burnt brightly.

This was exactly what I *didn't* want to happen.

Oh no, no, no, Tilly. You fool Issy, you shouldn't have told her.

I slapped my forehead. I had to play the diversion card. 'And, they liked my kickflip. It was hard doing it in the small space, but I nailed it!'

30

'That's cool,' Tilly mumbled as she stuffed a whole strawberry in her mouth. She wasn't the daintiest of eaters.

A smile came over my face.

Tilly looked at me. 'What are you smiling about?'

'Guess who asked me about my boarding afterwards?'

'Dunno, who?'

'Tim.'

'What? You're kidding!' Bits of strawberry exploded from her mouth, landing on my face. 'Oh sorry,' she said.

I wiped my cheeks and grinned. I could've been the Cheshire Cat's daughter.

'Sorry,' Tilly apologised and popped a double strawberry into her gob. I watched the juice droplets dribble down her chin. After swallowing it, she started to tease me. 'You go girl! Issy's got a boyfriend. Issy's got a boyfriend.'

'Stop it!' I giggled.

7:18 p.m.

Now I have to tell you that The Beast's reaction to my speech has angered me. In fact, it more than angered me, I'm outraged!

I revealed my secret, thinking she'd stop her name calling, once she knew why I had big eyes. But it didn't work and I don't know what to do now. Do I just put up with the bullying? I can't stop thinking that if I report her, or let Tilly report her, I could be her next victim. ☹

Tia, Tia you're so bad
Tia, Tia you make me mad.
Go away and leave me be
Go away and climb a tree!

You know, I really wish I could poke my eyes back into my head. That would solve the problem straight away. But I can't. ☹ I can't grow my hair so it covers my whole face or wear a paper bag over my head. There's no pill or miracle beauty cream that will help. It's *not my fault* I was born different!

Why is it that I was accepted for most of my primary school life, but now in high school I'm being bullied? Why is The Beast continuing, after I told the class why my eyes look the way they do? I know bullying is a power thing. She's trying to exert her power over me. I shouldn't let her get to me, but it hurts. It really *hurts*.

With this syndrome, my eyes are going to get bigger as I get older. (When I am eighteen I will have my last op to make me look 'normal'.) Does that mean more people are going to make fun of me? At the moment it's only the green-faced witch. Will there be more?

I wish I could snip The Beast up into miniscule pieces like confetti!

How am I going to get her off my back?

Chapter Four

Tuesday, 3 March

3:33 p.m.

OMG I've had a rotten, horrible, terrible day! Grrr... If I don't tell you what happened, I will punch something!

Problem No. 1:
Tilly invited this new girl to sit with us at first break. She doesn't normally do this, as we've always liked hanging out on our own; the Dynamic Duo, we call ourselves. So I didn't think too much of it. I was busy eating my ham and mayo sandwich when they arrived at our eating spot.

'Issy this is Sofia. Sofia, Issy.' Tilly made the introductions.

I mumbled a, 'Hi,' with my mouth full, and gave a wave.

I looked at the girl before me. I had never seen her before. She wore a chunky gold bracelet and diamond earrings.

Black shiny leather lace-ups clad her feet, and she had on a new and crisply ironed uniform. A French braid adorned her blonde head. When she opened her lunchbox she had a fancy real chicken and salad wrap and flavoured sparkling water.

I stared questioningly at Tilly.

'Ah, Sofia's new and doesn't know anyone,' she said.

'O-kay,' I said.

Tilly looked at me, raising her eyebrows.

Tilly began to talk to Sofia about their last period together which was Maths. I sat there, my brain starting to whirl; *Why is a rich girl coming to Pinnaroo High? What's her secret? There must be skeletons in her closet...*

I couldn't help it – I had to probe. I interrupted Tilly and her conversation about the boringness of solving equations; and something about William clowning around. 'What school were you at?'

Sofia turned towards me. 'Lady of the Divine.'

Ah, that's the expensive private Catholic school up the road. She does have money! What did she do to leave that posh school?

'Why did you change schools?'

'Bad grades.'

Tilly stared at me, her eyebrows tilted inwards. She was probably wondering what I was up to.

'Okay.' Was Sofia hiding anything? I looked at her for a while. I looked for any eye deflection, twitching of the lips or twirling of the hair. There weren't any.

'Why did you get bad grades?'

'Didn't do my assignments. Mum and Dad said they weren't paying for a private school education if I wasn't doing my work. I hated the school so I was happy to leave.' She shrugged. 'So now I'm here.'

'Oh. Do you know anyone here?'

'Only Taylah and Hunter who live in my street.'

I didn't know them so they must be in other grades.

'Okay.'

Tilly and Sofia continued their chatter and I sat quietly for the rest of the break.

*

Best friends are forever, yes that's true.
Best friends are forever, Tilly that's you.
No room for others, no others no way.
Just you and me together each and every day!

*

Problem No. 2:

While walking from D to G block, chewing over Sofia's arrival on the scene, and in my own little world, I was attacked. No it wasn't a Rottweiler, well maybe a human Rottweiler – it was *her*. 'Hey Fish Face, how's the pond today? Eaten any worms?'

Shock rocked me. I just stared into her self-satisfied 'you're too gutless to do anything about what I say' expression.

She knew she had me. I bet I looked like a stunned mullet. And she continued, 'Are you going in the swimming carnival Froggy Eyes? You must be good at doing the frog stroke.'

Now I'm not stupid. In fact I'm pretty intelligent. I realised at that moment that my speech had definitely failed. No ounce of being nice or having understanding lived in her. My speech had scored a big F for achieving its goal. The Beast had me by the throat. Did this new found intensity in the name calling mean I would cop it more? Did I really expect she'd change? Well yes, I actually did! Was that a dumb thing to expect? I didn't think so when I planned my speech… But I guess; do leopards change their spots? Do elephants lose their trunks? No! Maybe I was naïve.

After her attack, I stood rooted to the spot, my eyes as wide as saucers. I wanted to raise my fist and punch her right smack bang in her fat nose, but I couldn't. I didn't know if I had the guts to do it… and if I did, I would get a suspension.

So instead of being tough, I did my usual pitiful thing; put my head down and scooted. Her snigger reverberated inside my ears. 'Loser!'

My innards continued to bubble and boil with the invisible foam pouring out over the top of the pot. I stormed into the toilets and pushed the toilet door hard. It swung open and crashed against the wall. The sound echoed around the room. The girl in the adjoining stall yelled at me.

I didn't apologise which I normally would've done. I plonked down on the closed seat and tears filled my eyes, spilling down my cheeks.

Why is she so mean to me? Life is so unfair!

Problem No. 3:

The second break bell rang so I slunk out of the stall, washed my face and marched to my and Tilly's eating spot. I sat and waited and waited and waited. Tilly didn't arrive. I wondered where she was. Sofia didn't arrive either.

Has Sofia taken my best friend from me? Am I now all on my own?

I couldn't eat. Tilly, Sofia and The Beast all exploded in my head, like fireworks on New Year's Eve. I sat all alone, with my head down, drawing in my sketchpad so I didn't have to look at anyone who walked past me.

Where could she be? ☹

The last period dragged on. I watched the minute hand slowly move around the clock face. I wanted to see Tilly to find out where she'd been last break, and then go home and hide away in my bedroom, staying there until Jesus came back again.

Finally the three o'clock bell rang. I looked around for Tilly, and spied her with Sofia, deep in conversation, walking quickly towards the front gate.

What is going on? Why didn't she come to say bye to me? Has she dumped me?

Jealousy welled up in my heart. I wanted to run over to them and ask, but I couldn't. I don't know why. Instead I turned towards the back gate, and trudged the long way home, kicking every stick and stone that got in my way. LOSER ISSY! ☹

Be back later... I'm going to get myself a big bowl of ice-cream with chocolate syrup and sprinkles on top.

Maybe the ice-cream will make me feel better...

Chapter Five

6:41 p.m.

I ate my ice-cream (it didn't make me feel better but it was very yummy) and then hid back in my room. I sat at my dressing table and stared at my face in the large rectangular mirror. (You know, like the Queen in *Snow White*.)

Mirror, mirror on my dressing table, who's the fairest one of all? Me or Sofia? My hair's shoulder-length, dark brown and wavy. Sofia's is half way down her back, blonde and straight. My eyes are bulgy and green in colour. Nana always tells me they are like precious emeralds. I wish they were blue. Sofia's are small and pretty sky blue. I have many sun freckles; she has flawless skin. My cheekbones are flat; hers are high. My teeth are crowded; hers are straight. I'm a freak. She's a beauty. Mirror, mirror is that what you're telling me? Huh, that must be why Tilly wanted to be friends with her not me. ☹ What would any other reason be?

After dissecting my face, I flopped onto my bed and fixed my gaze on the glow-in-the-dark stars stuck to my ceiling. My eyes glazed over, as I went over the day. Suddenly I swore I heard my psychedelic longboard, which sat on the top shelf of my shoe stand, interrupt my cinema session, and whisper to me, 'Ride me Issy!' I know, that sounds really weird but I did! Or maybe I just imagined it... (All my skateboards were Christmas or birthday presents. And this is the order of them on my shelves: Top shelf = longboard; Second shelf = penny board; Third shelf = sneakers; Bottom shelf = ripstick.)

It was four-thirty so I had time. Boarding was my passion and I didn't need any excuse. I quickly changed out of my sweaty uniform, putting on a pair of faded denim jeans, a yellow hoodie t-shirt and purple sneakers. I strapped on my elbow and kneepads, and picked up my helmet, then tucked the whispering skateboard under my arm.

'I'm going to the skate park,' I told Mum as I walked through the kitchen, the aroma of freshly brewed coffee greeting my nose. She sat drinking her cuppa, doing the crossword in the back of the newspaper. Mum's always got her nose stuck in some type of puzzle these days. She says they'll keep away the dementia, whatever that means.

'Be home by five-thirty,' Mum replied without looking up. 'Ask your brother if he wants to go.'

'Oh Mum, why?' I didn't want him tagging along!

'Because if you don't, you won't be going.'

I sighed. I could tell by her tone of voice that she meant it, so I went to find Nathan. The bang, bang, bang sound led me to him in the backyard bouncing the basketball and shooting hoops. Of course he wanted to go. Grrr…

'Well hurry up. I'm leaving NOW!' I yelled.

I stuck my ear buds in, pressed my music app on my phone, and shoved my phone in my back pocket. I waited on the front steps. Nathan was quick.

9:38 p.m.

The skate park was behind the Pinnaroo Public Library. The council built it to get the kids off the streets, which worked for a while. Now only the die-hard boarders and the BMX riders frequented it. I liked that the park wasn't used by too many people. In the skate park there's a half-pipe, a mini ramp, a quarter pipe, a funbox which has a ramp and a rail, and some stairs. There's also a large flat area with an obstacle course with some small jumps for beginners. It's pretty good.

Nathan had brought his scooter. He went off to the obstacle course which meant he wasn't in my business. That pleased me. I headed to the mini ramp, going past the half-pipe. One day I'd venture onto it, but not yet. I was happy with the mini ramp. It was safe.

With my music pounding in my ears, I spent some time cruising from one side to the other, doing a backside grind. Freedom filled my body. It was as close to flying as I could get. If I could be a bird, I reckon I'd be an eagle or an albatross. Something big. Ha, then I could swoop and do a gigantic poop on The Beast's head. ☺

I glided over to the quarter pipe and worked on my frontside rock n roll. I misbalanced my board a few times, and stumbled down the ramp. With the number of operations I'd had on my head, falling worried me. I didn't want to land badly. An accident would be horrible, as I'd probably end up in hospital having another operation to fix the damage. Mum, Dad and my doctor would all be angry with me. I looked at my watch. Five-fifteen. Mum was pedantic about time. If we weren't home by five-thirty there would be a consequence.

'Come on Nathan it's time to go,' I called to him. He was playing on the small jumps.

As we walked in the door my watch said, five twenty-eight.
I looked at Mum. I could tell she was stuck on a clue by
the way she tapped the table furiously with her pen. She'd
have to wait until next week's paper to get the answer if
she couldn't figure it out. She wouldn't like that.

'We're back,' I announced.

She continued to tap and made no comment.

I lay on my bed and swiped my phone. I'd listen to
some music until dinner. There on the screen were three
missed calls and a message – all from Tilly.

Why didn't I hear the phone ring at the park?

I checked the sound. It was still on silent from class. I
changed it back, then stared at the screen.

*Should I ring her or listen to the message? Yes, No… Yes
I should because she's my best friend, versus, No I shouldn't
because she didn't say goodbye and she was with Sofia… Eeny
meeny miny moe… What am I going to do?*

My brain tossed back and forth like I was on a debating team.
My heart started to race and my hands became damp. My *anxiety*. ☹

I couldn't decide in this agitated state, so I did my
usual avoidance thing… I didn't call or listen, instead,
I dropped my phone down into my undies drawer. My
heart jumped as I thought I heard a crack. I looked at the
screen and let out a large sigh – the screen was fine. Mum
would've killed me if I'd broken it.

After dinner I again checked my phone. There were no more calls or messages. Curiosity filled my mind. I wondered what her message said.

I knew that all I had to do was type in 101, press call and listen to it, and I would know. But as I started to touch the numerals, 1 0, my heart started to speed like a V8 Supercar, zooming around the mountain at Bathurst, and my hands followed with their sweating.... I backspaced the numbers. Ugh. I just couldn't do it.

I wiped my hands on my t-shirt. I could try Facebook. She was probably on.

I looked at the Facebook icon on my screen... My heart thumped harder. Then my brain started; *But what if it's something bad, like she's going to tell me I'm no longer her friend? I bet that Sofia has snatched her away from me. That has to be it – there can't be any other reason...*

I threw my phone back in the drawer and stormed out of my room.

Mum, Dad and Nathan were laughing in the lounge room. They were watching a reality TV show where people do gross challenges to try and win money. I sprawled out on the soft leather recliner and Snowy jumped up onto my lap. I patted him and he went to sleep.

Maybe this show will take my mind off Tilly. It did a bit.

A movie came on which caught my attention. A guy and girl were trying to guess what flavours some chocolates were in a box, without reading the descriptions. They had to guess by looking at the shape and foil wrapping. If they guessed correctly, they ate the chocolate, otherwise the other person ate it. I thought about this for a bit – my brain got all deep for some reason. I thought up something pretty profound!

A box of assorted chocolates could represent people. The chocolate coating might be a person's hair colour, eye colour, skin colour and inherited diseases that are already in the DNA, being passed on from parents. That's why people say to Nathan, 'You look like your dad.' Nathan gets asthma. He got that from Dad too. But there are other things that can happen spontaneously – they're the middles of the chocolates – a surprise! Sometimes sweet, sometimes sour. That's how I see my Crouzons. I'm the first in my family. Mum and Dad were really shocked when I was born, as they didn't know I was going to have this syndrome. The milk chocolate they thought they were getting, had a nut centre.

Whoa I can't believe that came out of my brain… Pretty clever huh! But I haven't solved my Tilly problem.

I still don't know what to do. If she doesn't want me around anymore, I won't have anyone to hang with. That will give The Beast even more to tease me about. ☹

Chapter Six

Wednesday, 4 March

3:45 p.m.

I tossed and turned all night.

Could it be true that Tilly doesn't want me as her best friend anymore? Will she really want Sofia to be her bff?

I felt so miserable and stressed out, that there was no way I was going to listen to that message before going to school. I sulked over breakfast and slowly dressed so I would arrive at school just before the bell rang.

The closer I got to the school gate, the more worried I felt.

Have I lost my bff???

I went straight to my Form room. Whilst I stood there waiting for the teacher to arrive, Tilly bailed me up. Her first class was two blocks over, so she had obviously come looking for me.

She said, 'Issy why didn't you ring or text me back last night? I'm worried about you. I thought something had happened.' Her eyebrows were furrowed and her eyes dull,

I answered without thinking, 'I thought you were best friends with Sofia now.'

Tilly gave me a strange look. 'What? Didn't you listen to my message?'

'No.'

'Her father was in a car accident yesterday. He's bad. He's in ICU. She found out at three when her mum rang her. I walked her to her neighbour's car. Her neighbour took her to the hospital to see him! That's why I didn't say bye to you.'

'Oh.' I didn't know what else to say, so I studied my scuffed up sneakers, avoiding contact with her piercing brown eyes.

Tilly stuck her hands on her hips and explained, 'I rang to tell you. I even left a message so you'd know why I didn't say bye. I thought you'd at least text me back… And she's not my best friend – *you are!*'

I jerked my head up and crossed my arms in front of my chest, the jealousy and anger rising up in me. I could feel the tears behind my eyes. 'Well, where were you yesterday at lunch?' I said.

'I had detention.'

'You had detention? Why?' I think my eyes bulged even bigger. (Tilly's *never* had detention!)

'I back-chatted Sir in Maths.'

I couldn't believe it. 'Right. Since when do you back-chat teachers?' Before she answered, I asked her, 'Did you have detention with Sofia?'

'Yeah.'

I couldn't believe this either. I shook my head at her. The bell rang.

'See you at lunch,' Tilly said, jogging off to her class.

Maybe, maybe not.

Lunchtime came and I went to the Library. I sat on my own in a corner, pretending to read a book. To be honest, I didn't do much reading. The text blurred and I couldn't concentrate. I kept expecting Tilly to walk in through the door, so every time I heard the Library door open, I looked up to see who it was. But Tilly didn't come looking for me. My plan had backfired.

And this afternoon there have been no calls. ☹

8:30 p.m.

Still no more calls. Now I'm really worried. ☹

Have I lost my best friend? Is she now with Sofia? These thoughts keep whirling like a grinding garbage disposal unit in my mind.

What am I going to do?

I went on Facebook but she wasn't on. I didn't send her a message as I didn't know what to say. But I did see something I didn't like – she was now friends with Sofia. ☹

10:00 p.m.

Tonight Mum said I've been moody lately. So! She'd be moody too if she was me! ☹

3:12 a.m.

I can't sleep! I've been tossing and turning all night, watching my alarm clock tick on by. I can't get Tilly and the rich pretty girl out of my head. Ugh. What am I going to do?

Chapter Seven

Thursday, 5 March

6:50 a.m.

Great (sarcasm). Ugh, I feel like a bowl of squishy fish eyeballs. I'm so tired. I want to climb back into bed, pull the doona over my head, and teleport myself to my Island of Happiness. (My IoH would be a giant skate park at the beach or on a deserted island.)

On top of feeling tired, today is the school swimming carnival. I like swimming and I can swim well (which is why I like the beach) but I don't cope with racing where people watch you and rate your ability. You know, that *A* word. Swimming carnivals are a 12 for me.

I tried last year to work through my anxiety, but when I was waiting in the pavilion before my first race, it exploded like a supersonic nuclear meteor. My brain went psycho with a bombardment of questions ripping around it; *What if I drown? What if I come last? What if everyone laughs at me? What if the large scar on my head shows?* My heart pounded like a jackhammer and I was sweating a fountain. I got so worked up I spewed (I told you earlier in my journal that this had happened once – well this was when)… I was so embarrassed and of course I didn't swim as Mum came and picked me up.

Now I'm worried about what is going to happen today. Will it be Groundhog Day?

7:37 a.m.

It's seven thirty-seven and my hands are already sweaty. I'm ready. I'm wearing my yellow Flinders team shirt, and I've packed in my beach bag, my red and black full-piece swimmers, black rashie, goggles and Australian Flag beach towel. Oh I really want to stay home but I know Mum won't let me. There's no point asking her. She'll just say, 'You're a good swimmer Issy. You can do it.' It's going to be a bad day. I just know it. I DON'T WANT TO GO! ☹ *God help me.*

53

3:30 p.m.

Well, my thoughts this morning were correct. My day was awful. I should've stayed home, under my doona. Is God against me? I asked for help not a catastrophe. ☹

At the pool, my first problem confronted me straight away. Who to sit with? I looked at the sea of faces, already in the stands in front of me. Everyone seemed to be in their own little groups, and no one called out to me and said, 'Hey Issy come sit with us.' I spotted a space at the end of the third bench, beside some Year Eleven girls. Like a drop kick, all on my lonesome, I sat there, invisible.

I looked around. There was a sea of zinc cream painted faces, pom poms, rashies, shirts, boardies, swimmers, goggles and towels. I sat camouflaged in the stand with my team. The other team Cook, which Tilly was in, wore red.

It wasn't long and the first race was underway. 'On your marks. Get set,' said the HPE teacher. Beeeep went the horn. At least I could now watch the races and ignore the socialites around me.

Swimming carnival at the school.
Cook and Flinders in the pool.
Freestyle, backstroke, breaststroke, splash
Up the lanes the kids all dash.

✳

The Year Seven girls in their little bitty bikinis, dived into the crystal clear blue water. There was a belly flop, a nose dive, a huge splash, and a dash for panties to pull them back up, before they escaped to the bottom of the pool. The roar of cheering filled my head. Cook won, Flinders came second and third.

I knew it wouldn't be long and the teacher would be calling Year Nines to the marshalling area. Last year's fears came back like an erupting volcano; *What if I drown? What if I come last? What if people laugh? What if my head scar shows?*

I could feel a twisted knot forming in my belly. I needed Tilly. She's always helped me see things in perspective, stood beside me, supported me, and forced me to do the things I should do. Like when I didn't want to get up on stage, and act in a play in Year Seven. Like when I didn't want to give the class news on Assembly. Like when I didn't want to go and talk to the school librarian, when I lost my library book... Last year she'd been sick on the day of the swimming carnival.

55

I surveyed Cook in search of her. I found her – in the middle of the stand – chatting to Sofia. Sofia was there! They looked so happy together… Like besties… Maybe I'd been kicked to the curb. Invisible steam came out of my ears. Ughhh. ☹

'Year Nine girls for twenty-five metres freestyle come to the marshalling area,' boomed over the loud speaker.

My heart thundered in my chest, and my brain spun like a rapidly spinning merry-go-round. Sweat erupted on my forehead. I watched as the other Year Nine girls hopped up from the benches, took their team shirts off and skipped down the stairs.

What to do? What to do? Do I? Don't I? Can I? Can't I? whizzed and zoomed around my head.

It was decision time. No one cared I was there, so no one would know, or care, if I just sat there. I didn't want to go to marshalling and then spew like last year. That would be super mega embarrassing.

My eyes focussed on Tilly. I watched her stand up and edge along the metal bench to the stairs. She was going to race. If I went down there, I knew Tilly would stand with me so I could swim. Sofia had stayed in the stands so I didn't have to see her.

But the problem is I don't know why she didn't ring me yesterday or even if she's talking to me. She might be angry or

ignore me if I go down to marshalling. What will I do then?
☹ *Geez, if I had listened to the message on Tuesday night,*
or Facebooked her – then I wouldn't be in this predicament!

I pinched my wrist hard.

'Last call Year Nine girls for the twenty-five metres freestyle.'

I didn't move.

'On your marks. Get set.' Beeeep!

There went Tilly. I watched her dive like a duck, then follow the black line up to the end of the pool, touching the edge with her hand. Fourth. I watched her climb out of the pool, smooth her hair back, walk to her seat and high five Sofia. They started giggling. An angry black cloud settled in the pit of my stomach.

'Year Nine girls for twenty-five metres backstroke come to the marshalling area.'

'Last call Year Nine girls for the twenty-five metres backstroke.'…

'Last call Year Nine girls for the twenty-five metres breaststroke.' …

Tilly swam in all the races I should've been in. She came third, then second. I wondered if I'd swum, what I'd have come.

Would I have won a ribbon?

I'd never know… I sighed and scratched an L on my wrist.

'Year Nine girls for fifty metres freestyle come to the marshalling area.'

There weren't as many competitors in the fifty. But one of them was Sofia. She strolled to the marshalling area, looking glamorous in her Hawaiian floral bikini. Great (sarcasm). She was rich, glamorous and could swim. ☹

'On your marks. Get set.' Beeeep!

I watched Sofia do a perfect dive, then sail up the pool and back, to the starting blocks. She made it look so easy. *First!* Sofia swam in the rest of the races – Breaststroke. *First.* Backstroke. *Second.* Butterfly. *Fourth.* I detested her.

By three o'clock I was feeling like a dish of hot jalapeños – angry, jealous and confused. I sneaked out of the pool area after Tilly and Sofia had left so they didn't see me.

4:15 p.m.

I'm going to the skate park. Hopefully a ride will clear my head. My brother's watching TV, so I'm going to sneak out, so I don't have to take him. ☺

See ya later.

Chapter Eight

8:26 p.m.

Dad asked me over dinner how the swimming carnival went. I lied and told him I had swum, but didn't place. He told me I did a good job and how proud he was of me for facing my fears. Mum and Nathan were impressed too and congratulated me.

Why did I do that? I shouldn't have lied to Dad. I was a slimy eel to do that. ☹ He would be so disappointed in me, to know I'd fibbed. And now they all think I can handle my anxiety which I can't. ☹

After dinner, while I was washing up the dishes, the home phone rang. I looked around, but no one was coming to answer it. The caller ID said 'private number'. I quickly dried my hands on the hand towel and picked up the handset, thinking it was probably for Dad.

'Hi Issy.'

I caught my breath. It was Tilly. 'Ah hi,' I said to her.

'Did you go to the swimming carnival today? I didn't see you,' she said.

'Yeah.'

'Oh. You didn't swim?'

'No.'

'Issy, are you mad at me? You didn't sit with me at lunch yesterday or say bye.'

I didn't know what to say.

Should I say yes, or lie, and say no?

I said nothing.

She picked up on that. Tilly knew me so well. 'Why are you mad at me?'

'Because you like Sofia better than me!' There it was – the truth. Tears filled my eyes and my voice wobbled.

'I do not!' she exclaimed.

Then I let fly. 'Yes you do. I saw you with her at the swimming carnival. You two were having a great time! You didn't even notice I was there!' The tears slipped down my cheeks.

'You are my best friend Issy! Not Sofia. Don't cry.'

I started to get nasty then. 'Don't know about that.'

'I asked Sofia to sit with us because she doesn't know anyone. I thought you'd be okay with that. Sofia likes you. She thinks you're really nice. Issy *you are* my best friend – really. How can I prove it to you?' I knew she was trying hard to convince me. She was almost pleading.

'Tell Sofia to stop sitting with us.' There it was, I'd said it. I know I was being totally selfish, but I couldn't help it. Sofia was rich and pretty, she could go and find another friend quite easily. I couldn't.

'All right I will,' she said.

After I hung up, I had a yucky feeling in my gut, like I'd swallowed a plate of black sticky sludge. I hated fighting with Tilly. We hadn't had too many over the years, but when we did, I felt like part of me was being hacked off.

I wiped my face.

Dad came into the kitchen to make himself a cup of tea, and saw my red eyes, and tear stains. 'What's wrong Princess?'

'Nothing. PMS,' I muttered.

More lies. Ugh.

He didn't probe any further.

Friday, 20 March

7:22 a.m.

Tilly kept her word. She found another girl for Sofia to hang with. I don't know what reason she gave Sofia, but Sofia's been giving me strange looks. And you know what? I don't care. I need Tilly – Sofia doesn't.

I haven't said anything about them being friends on Facebook. I think that might be pushing things too far.

Tonight I'm staying over at Tilly's house. We decided during the week that it would be fun. We used to have sleepovers a lot in primary school. Mum thinks I'm just staying for the sleepover, but in actual fact that isn't totally true – it's a half-truth. As well as hanging out, watching movies and eating popcorn, Tilly *will* be colouring my hair. ☺ I can't change my face, but I can change my hair colour! I'm going blonde – don't they say blondes have more fun? ☺

Mum and Dad don't know this bit of information because when I wanted to put blue streaks in my hair last year, Mum's answer was, 'Not until you're eighteen.' And when I tried sucking up to Dad which normally works, he sided with Mum. So doing it this way, they won't know until it's done, and then it'll be too late.

Tilly has organised the stuff we need. She's bought the colour as well, so I didn't have to hide it at my place. Her mum colours her own, and Tilly's hair… so Tilly is confident she can do it. I can't wait to see the new me. ☺

Chapter Nine

Friday, 20 March

5:45 p.m.

Well, my awesome plans for my hair makeover today started stressfully, and had an *interesting*, I guess you could say, outcome. I'm still deciding on whether it was a good or bad decision to colour my hair… This is how it went down.

I was *so* excited about going to Tilly's, that I spent my last period, History, watching the minute hand going round on the wall clock above the whiteboard. As soon as we were dismissed at three o'clock, I walked straight to the front gate where Tilly and I were meeting up. She wasn't there, so I sat down beside the fence, and watched the other students race past, to do whatever they had planned for the weekend.

At three-ten there was still no sign of her.

At three-twenty there were only a couple of students left outside the gate. I looked at my phone. There was no missed call or message. This wasn't like her, so I went to Tilly's last lesson's room – Home Ec. I looked through the windows. The lights were off and the kitchen was empty.

Where is she? Did she go home without me? Is she with Sofia? Has something happened to her?

I thought I'd try the Admin building. Maybe she was there. I spoke to the receptionist behind the Welcome to Pinnaroo State High School counter:

'Has Tilly Watkins been in here?'

'No,' she said sharply, turning back to the pile of paperwork she was sorting through.

'Okay, thank you,' I said leaving the building. Outside the door, I plonked my bags down on the wooden bench and paced. The school was deserted except for a few teachers and the busy cleaners.

Where is she?

I clicked on her name on my contacts list. Her phone didn't even ring, but instead went straight to voicemail. I left a message, 'Tilly where are you? I'm at school waiting for you.' I waited, staring at the screen, expecting an instant call back.

There wasn't one.

After a couple of minutes, my hands started to get sweaty. I could feel my anxiety starting to kick in.

What am I going to do?

I tried to call her again. Ditto, it went to her voicemail. I pressed the 'end call' button.

It was obvious that she wasn't in the school, and I couldn't reach her on her phone... so there was nothing I could do... except... go home. I didn't understand it.

I dawdled towards the back gate. One last look around, but no Tilly anywhere. I stuck in my ear buds, turned on my music, and headed home.

I bet she's gone off with rich, beautiful Sofia.

As I crossed Morris Street, a small red car pulled up beside me. I didn't take any notice being wound up in my own little 'angry with Tilly' world.

'Issy!' caught my attention.

I stopped and looked at the car. I couldn't see through the reflection on the windscreen. Tilly's head popped out of the passenger's side window.

'Issy! Wait!'

I pulled out my ear buds.

Tilly jumped out, slammed the door and ran to me, blurting out, without as much as a breath. 'I'm so sorry. Mum picked me up early from school for an appointment. I forgot about it... and there was heaps of traffic... and my phone's flat so I couldn't ring you... and we only got back now!' She sucked in the air.

'Oh.'

Tilly grabbed my arm and started pulling me towards her car. 'Come on. We're going to do your hair.'

I slid into the back seat and stopped the song on my phone. I felt like a cow; my thoughts were wrong.

Tilly lives in Roland Street, on the other side of the railway. Most of the houses are brick with picket fences and bushy, flowery gardens in the front yard. Tilly has a pond in her front garden with goldfish in it – those huge orange ones. I like feeding them. I hold the bread in the tips of my fingers and they nibble it. They're cool. ☺

Tilly's Border Collie, Boots, came to meet us; barking and running in circles around the car. I opened the door, and Boots put his head inside, and sniffed me. I rubbed his head and said, 'Hey Boots.' He licked my leg with his wet and slobbery tongue. I got a whiff of him – *ew,* he needed a bath.

I followed Tilly inside. Her house looked the same – the semi-messy, lived-in look. It smelt the same, of lavender incense sticks.

'Come to my room,' Tilly said as she yanked me past the lounge room, then the kitchen, then the playroom, towards her bedroom. Tilly's door was closed. On the outside a sign said, 'Keep out or clean my room!'

'Do I have to clean your room?' I joked, shaking off my earlier feelings.

'Hmmm. Let me think about that for a minute?' Tilly joked back. 'Not tonight, but tomorrow before you go home.'

I poked my tongue at her and pushed the door open, going straight to Cheese's fish tank cage. Cheese is Tilly's grey pet rat. I took the mesh cover off, lifted him out, and sat him on my shoulder. He immediately ran up to the top of my head, and started nibbling my hair. His claws tickled my scalp.

'So you still want your hair done?' Tilly asked me, picking up my bags and placing them beside her bunk bed.

'Yes,' I told her. 'Have you got it?'

Tilly pulled out the hair colour from the desk drawer – Light Cool Blonde. I took the box off her and studied the picture on the front.

'I like it. The colour looks pretty. I'll look like Arisa.'

'Yeah, you will. Well let's see what we have to do.' Tilly took the box back off me. She tore the top flap and fished out the instructions.

I stood beside her and we read through them together. I could feel Cheese's whiskers tickling my forehead as he rebalanced himself. His tail wrapped around my ear.

'Did you get the stuff for it?' I asked her.

'Yeah.' Tilly left the bedroom and I followed her around as she collected a bowl, comb, box of gloves, Vaseline, two towels and some clips. We went back to her room and she set everything down on her desk.

'I think we're ready. Sit here,' Tilly instructed, pulling the study chair out from her desk.

She took Cheese off my head and popped him back into his cage. 'Cheese doesn't need to go Light Cool Blonde.'

'I thought he would rock with a blonde racing stripe down his back!' I teased. Tilly laughed. 'Are you sure you can do this?' I had to double check. There was no going back once she started.

'Yeah of course. I've watched Mum do hers and mine remember? It looks easy.'

'Okay, let's get started,' I said.

Chapter Ten

9:30 p.m.

Tilly wrapped a towel around my shoulders. It felt scratchy. She opened the jar of Vaseline and spread the goo across my forehead. Tilly looked very hairdresser-ish. I took a dollop out of the jar and smeared it on her cheeks.

'Hey,' she complained.

'You look so serious,' I teased her.

'Well I don't want to stuff it up.' Tilly said, waving her Vaselined finger at me.

'I don't want you to either!' (*Isn't that the truth?!*)

I watched Tilly as she opened the box of gloves and took three out.

'Maybe we can make some balloon animals later,' Tilly said as she began to blow one up, pretending to pop it in my ear.

I laughed.

She put the gloves on and poured the two bottles of product into the bowl. The mixture had a strong bleach smell.

'Okay, while that's activating I'll brush your hair,' she said picking her brush up off her desk.

'Why, is it a bomb?' I asked, trying to be funny. 'You know, like it's all combining to blow up?'

'Ha ha, that wouldn't be good. You have beautiful hair Issy,' Tilly told me as she brushed. 'It's much nicer than mine.'

'I like your honey blonde hair… and I like your copper streaks. Did your mum do them?'

'Yeah she did.'

'Your mum's cool,' I told her. Tilly's mum wasn't as strict as mine.

'Yeah she's good about the colouring. Okay, here we go. No changing your mind now.'

My tummy flip-flopped with excitement.

Tilly separated my hair into sections and applied the mixture. We were both quiet.

'Okay all done,' Tilly told me, taking off her gloves. I looked in the mirror. Not much to see.

'How long do we wait?' I asked her. The odour of the product wafted up my nose.

Tilly read the box. 'Um, thirty minutes.'

'Okay. Hope I can last that long with the smell.' I pinched my nose with my thumb and finger.

'You'll get used to it,' she said. 'What do you want to do while we wait?'

'Draw?' I suggested.

'Sounds like a plan.' Tilly said.

I pulled my pencil tin and sketchpad out of my overnight bag. 'What do you want to draw?'

'How about portraits of each other?' Tilly said.

I laughed. 'All right.' I worked on my portrait of Tilly. I gave her wild ruffled hair, a rock pantsuit and a star-shaped bass guitar.

I held it up to her.

'That's cool Issy. Can I pin it on my board?'

'Sure. How am I going?' I asked, trying to sneak a look at her sketchpad.

'You can't see it yet!' Tilly retorted with a giggle, turning her back on me.

I started on another picture – me as Arisa.

A few minutes later, Tilly spun around with a, 'Ta da.'

On the paper a female caricature with a mop of spiky hair, tatts covering her arms and piercings in her nose, stared back at me.

'I like that,' I chuckled. 'I'll take it home to Mum and see what she thinks.'

Tilly snorted. I chuckled louder at her snort. We both collapsed in fits of laughter. ☺

Our drawings consumed us.

I thought Tilly had set the alarm on her phone, but apparently not, as when I asked her, 'How long's it been?' she checked and replied with, 'Geez, forty-five minutes. We better wash your hair now! Come into the laundry and we'll wash it in the tub.'

'Didn't you set the alarm?' I asked her.

'I thought I did,' she said, as we hurried to the laundry.

I wasn't stressed until Tilly rinsed my hair under the tap and I heard her gasp. Instantly my heart went boom, boom, boom.

'What's wrong?' I asked her.

'Geez… nothing!' Tilly stammered.

Her voice had risen. I knew instantly that something was wrong.

'I don't believe you!' I said, standing up. My voice raised.

I headed straight to the mirror. I stared at my reflection. Yep, that was me but look at my hair – it wasn't Light Cool Blonde – it was a scary shade of dirty orange!

'Oh no, Tilly! How did that happen?' I cried.

She came and stood behind me.

I turned towards her. Tears welled in my eyes. 'I thought you knew what you were doing.'

'I thought I did. Sorry Issy. Let's shampoo it right now.'

I stripped off as fast as I could and jumped into the shower. I shampooed and shampooed and shampooed. The bottom of the shower filled with fluffy foam and apple blossom scent filled my nose.

Turning off the shower taps, I prayed. *Dear God. Please let my hair be blonde like I wanted.* I didn't want to look, but I had to. I tentatively rubbed the steam off the mirror. There was my reflection. What colour was my hair? A lighter shade of dirty ORANGE. *OMG.* A few not nice words escaped from my lips.

Tilly came into the bathroom to see.

'I'm *really sorry* Issy.' Her voice quivered. 'I didn't mean to stuff it up.'

'What are we going to do?' I said. I wanted to bawl. Why didn't anything in my life go right?

'Let's get on YouTube and see if there's something we can do to fix it.'

Tilly turned on her laptop.

Chapter Eleven

10:04 p.m.

All on-line researching led to the fact that my hair couldn't be re-coloured for a few days. I fell back on Tilly's bed – my life was over! I covered my face with my hands.

'It doesn't look that bad Issy. You look… distinguished… like Nicole Rickfield,' Tilly said.

I grimaced under my hands.

That was a lovely thing for her to say. Nicole Rickfield was a beautiful actress with red hair. (I guess she was trying to make a tree frog out of a cane toad.)

I uncovered my face to see Tilly picking up her pillow. She hit me with it and grinned. In retaliation, I grabbed my pillow.

'Pillow fight!' I yelled at her, smacking her in the head.

Tilly's mum, came to investigate the noise. She looked at my hair.

'That's not blonde Issy. Did you get another colour?'

'No, it was supposed to be blonde,' I told Mrs Watkins.

'We left it on too long,' Tilly piped up sheepishly.

Tilly's mum frowned at her. 'Did you try washing it out?'

'Yep, but it didn't work,' Tilly said.

'Oh. What's your mum going to think?' Mrs Watkins asked me.

'I'm probably going to be grounded for life.'

'Hmmm,' was her final comment before she left the room. The door shut quietly behind her.

Saturday, 21 March

Midday

Well, Mum's reaction met my expectations. 'Oh my goodness Isabella Marie! What have you done to your hair?' Her face was as white as a ghost. I really thought she might faint.

'Tilly coloured it blonde but it turned out orange.'

Tilly stayed silent beside me, trying to look all sweet.

'You let her?' she asked me with her, 'are you stupid' look on her face.

'Yes,' I said, while I thought; *Well Mum she didn't tie me down with duct tape.*

'Why?' she wanted to know.

'Because I didn't want brown hair anymore. I wanted blonde hair.'

'Well that's not going to happen. I'll make an appointment with the hairdresser,' Mum snapped.

'Can she colour it blonde for me?' *It's worth a try.*

'No Isabella. It's going back to brown. We'll talk more about this when we get home.'

As Mum marched me out to the car I twisted and gave Tilly my peace sign.

3:47 p.m.

I've spent the day in my bedroom. Mum and Dad have decided on my punishment. I'm grounded to my room for a week with no phone and Internet. I thought it would be more severe than that.

For the past fifteen minutes I've been looking at myself again in the mirror. No mirror, mirror this time. I've been checking out my new hairdo. Now I've calmed down, I actually like the orange. Maybe I should leave it this way. It's so out there it would definitely take the attention away from my eyes. Other girls have red... I need to think of what to say to convince Mum.

Snip, snip, colour, foil.
Looking like a gargoyle.
Style, style, spritz, spray.
Pretty fancy, I must say!

Sunday, 22 March

8:16 p.m.

I tried yesterday afternoon to persuade Mum to let me keep my hair colour but the more I tried, the crankier she got. I backed off when she threatened me with an extension of my grounding. ☹

Let's see how things go at school tomorrow. I might want my hair to go back to brown ASAP. I don't know whether I'm scared or excited!

Saturday, 28 March

8:00 a.m.

I was very nervous as I entered the school gates. My hands were clammy. In my bag, I had a beanie, just in case I needed to hide my hair. If people got mean, I would be shoving it on. But as it turned out, I didn't need the hat. In fact an amazing thing happened – I was a human magnet for other Year Nine girls who'd had hair colouring disasters themselves. ☺

At every class I was told stories by girls who normally didn't talk to me. Some girls even complimented me on the colour, saying orange suited me and that I should keep it. (And I don't think they were being sarcastic.) What I really liked was that I was noticed for something other than my face, and I actually felt popular for the first time in my life... It was wonderful. ☺ This must be how the cool kids feel.

Of course the evil curse also noticed. I copped The Beast's, 'Hey Goldfish. Hey Red Frog.' More barbs, but to be honest, they didn't hurt as much as usual. I think all the great things the other people said and the fact that so many girls spoke to me, were more important than her name-calling, so I didn't take as much notice of her as I normally do. ☺

4:35 p.m.

This afternoon I went to the hairdresser. I tried one more time to have it coloured blonde but Mum put her foot down and wouldn't budge... so my hair is now brown again. Thanks Mum. *Not.*

I'm off for a board. Talk to you later.

Chapter Twelve

Monday, 30 March

3:45 p.m.

I received a pink envelope today from Tilly. It had my name on it in hot pink curly writing.

'Open it!' Tilly squealed.

I turned the envelope over. A silver dolphin sticker sealed the flap – Tilly's favourite animal. Inside was a piece of decorative notepaper.

You are invited to Tilly's fabulous 14th Birthday Party

Where: Pinnaroo Laser Zone

When: Saturday 11 April

Time: 5-8pm

RSVP: 7 April

'You're having a party!' I exclaimed. Tilly didn't normally have birthday parties. The last time would have been at Macca's when she was seven.

'Yeah I am!' she shrieked, jumping up and down.

'I'm coming!' I squealed, jumping up and down too.

'It's going to be fun. I'm gonna shoot you!' Tilly shot me with her finger, making a bang noise.

I held my chest and dramatically collapsed to the concrete. Tilly pulled me back up. The bell rang so we went our separate ways.

I can't wait. I haven't been to anybody's birthday party since Shelby's Princess Pamper Party in Year Five. ☺

Woot woot let's celebrate
Tilly's birthday will be great
Cake, candles, laser tag
Streamers, presents, a party bag.

Saturday, 11 April

9:05 p.m.

Well, the party would've been awesome, if Sofia hadn't been there, and if she hadn't given *my* Tilly *that* gift. I'm really spewing about *that* gift. ☹

You see, it had taken me heaps of effort to find the perfect present for Tilly. I'd planned what I wanted to buy her and I'd trawled through seven stores searching for it. I wanted to buy her a sterling silver necklace with a dolphin pendant. In frustration and running out of time, I was just about to give up, when I found one at the store, Silver Elephant. The necklace was perfect. It even had a tiny diamond for the dolphin's eye. I stared at the pendant in its blue box before I wrapped it in brightly coloured Happy Birthday paper, finishing it off with a silver bow. I couldn't wait to see Tilly's reaction. I was certain she would love it.

When I arrived at the party there were only a couple of other kids, Torey and Ben. Tilly gave me a huge hug and I gave her the present. I watched her face expectantly as she untied the ribbon, tore off the paper, and opened the jewellery box.

'I love it Issy. Thank you!' she told me, squealing, clutching the necklace to her chest. That's what I'd hoped for. ☺

'Put it on me,' she instructed.

I fastened the necklace around Tilly's neck, flicking her hair out of the way. I watched her as she fondled the pendant. The tiny diamond sparkled from the lights of the room. The necklace stood out beautifully against her black top. Yes, I did a good job. The others were arriving but none of their presents were as awesome as mine. ☺

All was going perfectly, until the door to Laser Zone opened and *she* was there standing in the doorway. I didn't even know that Tilly had invited her.

'Happy birthday Tilly,' Sofia sang, handing over a gold holographic gift bag. Well that meant the invitation went to her too. ☹

I watched Tilly intently as she took out a small white box with a pink ribbon on top.

'I hope you like it!' Sofia cried.

Tilly opened the box, let out a high pitched scream, and bent forward. I craned my neck around Torey. Lying on a pixie-sized white pillow a pair of diamond stud earrings sparkled. Whoa! The diamonds were three times the size of the one on the dolphin pendant.

'They're real diamonds and white gold,' Sofia stated. 'Do you like them?'

Tilly stared at Sofia, her eyes as big as saucers.

'Yes I LOVE them!' she yelled, hugging Sofia tightly.

'Issy look at the earrings. They're *diamonds*!'

'They're beautiful,' I muttered.

My brain started to whirl; *Why did she invite Sofia? Why didn't she tell me? Why did Sofia have to come? Why did Sofia have to buy diamond earrings? Will Tilly like Sofia more than me now?*

I sat and sulked. Tilly ignored me, absorbed in her celebrations. I felt like cat vomit. ☹

The time came for laser tag. I didn't fancy playing. Everyone else had gone to the area where you get all suited up. I continued to sit at the table.

'Come on Issy.' Tilly came back and pulled my arm. 'You'll have fun.'

'I don't want to play,' I mumbled.

She kept pulling me. I had no choice.

Grasping my laser gun, I moved with the others into the game room.

'I'm gonna shoot everyone,' Tilly teased, waving her gun about at her friends.

'I'll get you,' Tyson retorted, pointing his gun back at her.

After the attendant's instructions everyone scattered.

Tilly yelled, 'I'm gonna get you all! Watch out!'

My heart skipped and goose bumps rose on my arms as I watched everyone flee. I stayed where I was - alone. I really didn't like the idea of shooting people.

What am I going to do? I don't want to do this. It reminds me of hide-and-seek which I don't like playing either. Maybe I should just leave...

I wiped my sweaty hands on my pants and stared into the semi-darkness. My brain began to do its usual; *Will I? Won't I?*

Ahead of me, about ten metres away, I could see a shape – like someone was lying on the floor behind a large box. They were on their stomach and facing the other way.

All I have to do is laser them. It's just like a water pistol. It won't be that hard. It won't hurt them.

My heart thumped as I tiptoed closer. My victim hadn't heard me so it was easy to aim at their back. My trembling finger pressed the trigger. Zap! Their vest lit up.

The person sat up and stared at me. 'Who? What? Issy,' he complained.

'Sor...sorry, Adam,' I stuttered, not knowing what else to say.

Adam rose and disappeared into the darkness. We all had three chances.

My brain felt happier.

That wasn't so bad. In fact it was kind of fun. Better than I thought it would be. Where's my next victim?

I crept around and saw another prone silhouette. Only the white soles of the shoes glowed. I pointed my gun and pressed the trigger, hoping it would hit its target. Zap!

'Hey,' Ben protested sitting up, surprised by my ambush.

'Got ya!' I grinned at him. It was becoming real fun now! I tiptoed onwards.

Zap! *No way. That's me.*

I spun and peered into the shadows.

It better not be Sofia…

Chapter Thirteen

9:41 p.m.

Tilly's face grinned at me in the gloom of the laser tag room.

'Hey, you're not supposed to shoot your bestie,' I complained.

'Sorry. You shoot me now,' she told me. 'Go on.'

'But I'm dead. I can't,' I protested.

'Doesn't matter. Shoot me Issy.'

'Okay; the ghost of Issy will shoot you,' I said in a wafting ghostly voice.

We both giggled.

I aimed my gun at her chest and placed my finger on the trigger…

'Got ya Tilly!' Sofia cried out.

What? I dropped my gun to my side. 'Witch,' I mumbled, scowling.

Sofia and Tilly laughed.

I stomped towards the exit. A fountain of hot lava pulsed in my head.

'Issy...' I heard from behind me.

I didn't turn back. It didn't matter that I had two more chances. I kept on going out to the café area.

I thought Tilly would follow me, but she didn't. I sat at one of the tables in Tilly's designated area, and munched on some chips that were in a dolphin shaped plastic bowl. Torey tried to talk to me. Out of politeness I made some conversation. Inside my heart, the San Andreas Fault Line was cracking open.

I don't even know who won the game.

Not long afterwards, everyone gathered around the birthday girl and sang Happy Birthday. Tilly cut her dolphin-shaped cake, hitting the bottom, which meant she could kiss the nearest boy, who just happened to be Sam – her secret crush. He blushed. She blushed. That would've made her happy. Normally I'd have teased Tilly about Sam, and even celebrated with her that she stole a kiss... but not tonight.

We played the video games. I lost at everything. I kept hearing Sofia's ugly voice as she played alongside Tilly. It filled the air like rotten egg gas. At eight o'clock I happily left. It was supposed to have been a great night celebrating Tilly's birthday, but Sofia ruined it. ☹

Dad asked me in the car, 'Princess, did you have a good time?'

'Yeah.'

I didn't want to tell him. I pinched my wrist hard.

I feel like I'm losing my best friend and I don't know what to do about it. I don't know what to do about anything in my life. I'm so confused. My life is a bowl of poo. ☹

Monday, 20 April

5:50 p.m.

Tilly's birthday was the last Saturday before the Easter holidays, so I hadn't been able to talk to her about the presents. My family went camping at Mt Samson for a week, and then Tilly's family went to the Sunshine Beach Holiday Park for a week. So today, I had planned on asking her. I intended on being calm. I didn't want to fight, but I think it had been simmering for too long and things didn't go so well. ☹

Basically, as soon as I saw Tilly I noticed the necklace and earrings. The rage monster in me instantly came out.

I attacked her with, 'Tilly do you really like my necklace?'
My voice was a bit high pitched. (I don't think I even said,
'Hi' or 'How was your holiday?')

'Yes I do! It's beautiful Issy. Dolphins are my favourite
animal. Why?' She looked confused.

'I thought you might like Sofia's earrings more. They
obviously cost a lot more money,' I spat at her.

'Issy, I love her earrings too. I've never had diamond
earrings before.' Her voice was high pitched.

'Why didn't you tell me Sofia was going to the party?'
There I said it.

'I did!' Tilly's eyes were wide open.

'No you didn't. What else haven't you been telling me?'
I asked her.

'Nothing. I swear I told you.' Her hands went on her hips.

'No you didn't,' I spat.

'What's going on Issy? Why are you so upset?' She was
frowning at me.

I spun and stormed off without answering her. I know
that was babyish of me, but that's what I did.

'Issy!' I heard behind me.

At lunchtime we sat together, but in angry silence. (I
didn't go to the Library.)

Tilly tried to explain again. 'Issy, I did tell you I
invited her.'

But I didn't agree. 'You're lying. I'd have remembered that important bit of information,' I said.

I really don't remember her saying that at all.

Tilly sighed. More angry silence. The bell rang and we went our separate ways.

7:00 p.m.

My life's so sucky. ☹ Tonight I'm just going to stay in my room, listen to my music, and play games on my computer.

Chapter Fourteen

Tuesday, 21 April

4:15 a.m.

After another night of rotten sleep and trying to count rams (you know instead of sheep), I've been thinking some random questions; *What's the point of life? Why are we here? Is it to go to school, and then work until you drop dead? Is it to get married and have kids? Is it to have faith in God? Is it to do good things like Mother Teresa? Or, is it to fight with your best friend???* ☹

Why can't things just be how they were last year? I hate fighting! I just want Tilly to myself.

Tuesday, 28 April

5:10 p.m.

The week's been long. Tilly and I are talking but there's still a bit of tension between us. I know she thinks I'm being stupid about the gifts…and Sofia… and maybe I am, but I can't help it.

Wednesday, 29 April

4:23 p.m.

At school today we were talking about careers. What do I want to do after school? I don't know. Sometimes I think it'd be fun to be in the X-treme Sports Skateboarding Team, but I don't think I'd ever be good enough. ☹

Thursday, 30 April

5:49 p.m.

This afternoon I sneaked out of the house again, without telling Nathan. He was in his bedroom with his door closed. I took Snowy with me instead. Snowy likes to run around the obstacle course and he's just so cute with his floppy ears bouncing. I sat on the concrete step, patting him, with my skateboard beside me, and gazed at the half-pipe. I imagined myself riding from side-to-side. I saw crowds of people applauding me as I bowed. Me, Issy Burgess, *a skateboard champion*. I'd even have my own Twitter following and media interviews. I'd be famous. ☺

As I was lost in my own little magical world, there came a voice, 'Hi Issy.'

'Issy? Hi.' It came again, as I reoriented myself into reality.

Huh? I twisted to my left, up into the face. Tim! *OMG.* Whoa, my heart began to bang.

'Hi,' I said, smiling.

'Watcha doing?' he asked casually. He reached down and patted Snowy. 'Cute dog. Is he yours?' Snowy licked his hand.

'Yes. This is Snowy.' I picked Snowy up and gave him a cuddle. 'Just daydreaming about the half-pipe. I want to ride it one day.' I sounded so calm, but inside my stomach swished like a washing machine.

'Want me to show you how?'

I stared at him. *What? You can board?*

I said, 'You can ride it?'

'Yep. I'll show ya.' I watched as Tim took off his black cap and handed it to me. I pinched myself – it wasn't a dream.

I stared at Tim as he glided to the half-pipe, climbed to the top and perched on the coping. I sat spellbound. I had no idea he was even into boarding, let alone that he could do this. As Tim strapped on his helmet I admired his athletic figure through his Nike SB t-shirt. I noticed his sneakers – they were Vans - how I'd love a pair of them! ☺

'Ready?' he called.

'Go!' I smiled.

I watched Tim roll down and up to the other side. *Wow.* He took a bow. I clapped. He rolled back, jumped down and sauntered over to me, carrying the board. Tim took off his helmet and my heart melted. His eyes glittered like crystals. OMG, he was so adorable.

'That was awesome!' I said, trying to keep myself together.

'What are you working on?' Tim asked as he sat down on my concrete step. The denim of his shorts brushed my leg and I smelt his cologne mixed with boy sweat.

'A few things. I'm a bit hit-and-miss on my frontside rock n roll and I'm trying to do a 270. I can do a 180,' I said.

'I can do those. Do you want some help?'

I couldn't believe what I was hearing. 'Um, yes, that would be great.' It felt like I had Mexican jumping beans bouncing in my belly. I hoped I didn't sound desperate.

'Great, let's go.' He stood up.

We rolled over to the quarter pipe, with Snowy scampering beside us.

'Show me what you can do,' Tim directed. 'Show me your rock n roll.'

'Okay.' I tied Snowy's lead to the scaffolding. I patted him and he lay down.

I strapped on my helmet and took off, rolling up the pipe. My stomach flip-flopped as I rocked my board on the lip of the coping. I had to get this bit right. As I tried to turn the board to roll back down, I felt my foot lose its traction on the board and I stumbled down the slope. The board rolled ahead of me, stopping under Tim's foot. I felt my cheeks redden with embarrassment. I could do this.

'I can do it,' I mumbled.

He nodded. 'Good try. Do you want to do it again?'

'Sure.'

I wanted to make it, to show him I could do it, but I lost my footing and stumbled down the ramp again.

'I don't know what I'm doing wrong,' I told him. 'I've watched plenty of YouTube videos but I can't seem to stick it very often.'

'Let me show you.' Tim said strapping on his helmet. 'You're very close.'

I moved beside the ramp and watched Tim perform the trick to perfection. (He was my dream guy.) ☺

He stood back at the foot of the ramp. 'Come over here,' he said.

I rolled over.

'Let's go through it step by step,' he said. 'I'll show you what you're doing wrong.'

'Okay,' I said, my stomach feeling like a fully wound up jack-in-the-box.

Chapter Fifteen

6:30 p.m.

Tim and I spent the next hour working on my frontside rock n roll. He broke it down into the trick's steps, showing me where I needed to place my feet. I giggled every time I messed it up. Each time Tim would smile and patiently say, 'Let's do it again Issy.' Those crystal eyes held me in their trance and I wanted the lesson to last all afternoon.

After about the tenth attempt I stuck the trick.

'Yay!' I fist pumped the air and high fived Tim.

'Cool, Issy,' he congratulated me.

'Thank you. You're a great teacher.'

I saw a pink flush on his cheeks. 'You just had your front foot in the wrong place.'

I smiled and took off, sticking it one more time.

Tim followed me.

We stopped on the path near the ramp. I suddenly realised I hadn't been watching the time. If I was late home I wouldn't be allowed to come back to the skate park for a while. I didn't want that. I wanted to see Tim more.

I looked at my watch. 'Oh, I have to go home now,' I said feeling awkward.

'Okay, me too. See you at school.' And he skated off in the opposite direction.

I ogled his back as he disappeared out the rear gate. I untied Snowy and rode home.

*

The concrete curves into the air
Falling off gives a scare
Kickflip, 180, rock n roll tricks
I love it when my skateboard sticks.

*

Mum noticed my humming as I made myself a glass of Milo. I put five heaped teaspoons of the crunchy brown powder on top of the milk. Mum was chopping the mushrooms and capsicums for the risotto we were having for dinner. The air smelt of onions. She stopped mid chop and raised her eyebrows at me. 'Did something happen at the skate park?'

'Yep, I mastered the frontside rock n roll.' I grinned.

'That's wonderful.' She smiled. 'You're being careful aren't you?'

'Thanks and yes.'

'You went to the skate park?' Nathan asked me, looking unhappy. He was getting some biscuits out of the cupboard. Mum frowned at him.

'Yep,' I said.

'Why didn't you tell me?' he grumbled.

I ignored him and walked off towards my room. I knew Mum had no clue what I was talking about. She'd never been interested in coming to the park to watch me board. She had no clue about the tricks I could do. Part of me didn't care but the other part wished she did.

And... no way was I going to tell her anything about Tim. He was *my* secret. ☺

6:40 p.m.

I didn't want to tell Mum but I had to tell Tilly. I typed her name into my phone and pressed the call button.

'Hi. I have some news!' I told her excitedly.

'What?' There was a spark in her voice.

'I went to the skate park this afternoon and Tim was there, and he helped me with my tricks.'

Tilly squealed. 'Woot woot Issy.' With that squeal I knew things were all better between us. *Yay!* ☺

'Oh, he is *so* cute.' I smiled as I remembered our afternoon.

'I didn't know he skateboarded,' Tilly said.

'I didn't either. He didn't tell me when I did my talk.'

'Is he going to give you more lessons?' I could hear some teasing in her voice.

'Don't know. We didn't talk about more lessons.'

Oh, I so much hope so.

'Hey, did you see the flyer about the X-treme Sports Skateboard Team?' she asked me.

'No. What are they doing?' *That was exciting news – the X-treme Sports Skateboard Team!*

'They're coming to school next week. The flyer is up near the Tuckshop.'

'Really? I didn't know that. Oh that's fantastic! Maybe I can meet them.'

Was this God? Yesterday I was thinking about my career, and now I'm going to see them.

'Get on Skype so we can talk more. I'm running out of credit on my phone,' I told her.

We continued our chat about playing laser tag and Sam's kiss. Neither of us mentioned Sofia. Then we moved onto other stuff.

In bed I relived the afternoon. I could see Tim's beautiful eyes. His soft hair. His cute dimples... I could smell his cologne. I could hear his adorable chuckle. I wrote Tim on a piece of paper with my felt pens. (I drew a heart on top of the 'i'.) I sprayed some rose scented body spray on the note and placed it under my pillow.

9:15 pm

Happiness is pulsing through my veins. Tilly and I are back to our old selves, Tim is just so lovely. I think my crush has become a mega crush... and I'm going to see the X-treme Team. *Thank you God.* ☺ I feel like a little girl on Christmas Eve. Will I be able to sleep tonight? Lah, lah, lah!

Chapter Sixteen

Monday, 4 May

4:17 p.m.

I talked to Tim on the way to Science, about our new English assignment we'd just been given by Miss O'Keefe. He didn't mention yesterday afternoon so neither did I... And yes, I definitely have a mega crush. ☺

I stood beside him while we waited for the door to open. The Beast, in front of us, turned around, screwed up her face and eyeballed me. I tried to pretend I didn't see her silent threat. Inside me, my nervous stomach leaped.

Later in the day we had Maths. I'd sat down in my chair and was getting my laptop ready. I wasn't taking any notice of who was walking past me, when I heard in my ear, 'Flathead, get your bony fingers off Tim. He's mine.'

'Go-o-o a-way,' was all I could stutter. My brain scrambled to process what she had just said – don't talk to Tim?

'You heard me,' she whispered, then walked to the back of the room.

What? She doesn't want me to talk to Tim?

The vision of The Beast glaring at me outside the Science Lab, after I had done my speech, and then today, came back to me.

Oh no, she likes Tim too.

God, can't she just go away, move schools, pick on someone else or something?

Does this make Problem No. 4? The Beast has the hots for the same boy I do… How do I solve that???

I need to get out of here. I'm going to the skate park (maybe Tim will be there ☺).

8:45 pm

Tim wasn't at the park, ☹ but I definitely have mastered my frontside rock n roll. ☺ Tomorrow the X-treme Team is coming to school – I can't wait. I hope I get to meet them.

Tuesday, 5 May

3:41 p.m.

I HATE HER!

The Beast captured me again today. I was minding my own business, as normal, walking between Science and HPE. I turned the corner of the Library and ran right, straight, smack, bang into *her*. She dug her fingers into my shoulders, and stared into my frightened eyes. I smelt the garlic bread she'd eaten.

'How's it going Pug? (Another new name. Has she googled *animals with big eyes* or something?) Didn't see you drown yourself at the swimming carnival,' she whispered.

I felt my face turn a dark shade of red and I tried to speak, but like a ventriloquist doll without its puppeteer, I said nothing.

She then pushed me roughly into the wall and snickered. 'Too gutless to even talk to me. You better not be talking to Tim either. He's mine.'

I hit the painted besser blocks as she walked away. My hand stung.

'Ow!' I snapped, shaking it.

A friendly voice spoke to me. 'Issy, you all right?'

'Um, yeah.' It was Tilly.

'What's wrong?' she wanted to know.

'Nothing. Just hurt my hand.' (That was true.) I continued to shake my hand, as I put my face back into my 'everything's okay' expression, hoping she'd think the redness was due to my hand. I didn't want to tell her what had just happened. I didn't want her to make matters worse.

Anyway my excuse must've worked, as she grabbed my arm. 'Come on, the X-treme Team is setting up.' She led me towards the back oval.

I should've been excited about the X-treme Team. I'd been impatiently waiting for this moment. But now I just wanted to curl up in a ball, like an echidna, and stick people with my spines.

In front of us, on the running track, six guys were finishing up the construction of a wooden half-pipe, and a couple of guys were standing around watching the kids arrive. The guys were all wearing black t-shirts and pants. The words *X-treme Sports* were emblazoned on their clothes and on the side of the large truck parked nearby. Rock music blared from the sound system.

Kids were filling the oval. The music drawing them. Some were popping and dancing, others doing handstands and generally showing off. The atmosphere was full of fun and anticipation. I suddenly felt excited.

This is what I've been waiting for. This is my chance to meet some real life pro-skateboarders. This is my dream! This is what I want to do one day. Will there be a girl?

A wave of eagerness rose up inside me. *This is going to be awesome.*

We sat on the prickly grass and waited for things to get underway. The sun was warm. Navy uniforms were filling the patches. I noticed Sofia chatting away with some girls and guys. She had obviously made other friends quite easily.

'There's Tim over there,' Tilly pointed out.

'Yeah,' I said, feeling a blush coming on.

'Ask him to sit with us!' she said to me.

'No!' I scanned the crowd for The Beast. I couldn't see her.

'Okay, I will.' And she called out to him. 'Tim, over here.'

Tim turned in our direction. I put my face down, and stared at my crossed legs. She beckoned for him to come over to us. He did.

'Hey. Do you want to sit with us?' Tilly asked him.

'Um, no sorry, I'm over there with Sam and Dylan.' I let out a breath. 'Issy, this is going to be cool huh?'

I raised my head and nodded. 'Yep.'

'Well, see ya later,' and Tim wandered off.

I groaned and fell back on the grass.

'He likes you,' Tilly teased me.

I didn't mention The Beast's threat to Tilly.

The music stopped and the microphone crackled. 'Hey guys, welcome to X-treme Sports. Today we're proud to present to you our skateboarding team.' I sat back up.

Each of the guys was introduced... And one of them was a girl. Sarah McGrath. Yes! Now I was seriously eager to see what she could do. ☺

Tilly nudged me. 'That could be you one day,' she said.

'I'd love that.'

'You need to go and say hello to her afterwards,' she encouraged.

I sat entranced by the guys' prowess. The tricks they did were unbelievable - ollies and flips, slides and grinds, air and grabs, lip, hand and foot plant tricks. One after the other, the tricks came thick and fast. I sat engrossed.

These were all tricks I had studied on YouTube and here they were doing them!

I watched as Sarah took the stand next, posing on the coping with her board. I wondered what trick she was going to do. I had studied female skateboarders on YouTube too. Some of them did amazing tricks. My eyes followed her as she rolled down and up, then executed a perfect 540 in the air. I yelled and clapped until my hands were red and stung. Others whistled.

Sarah then performed a 360 kickflip with one of the guys. That was something I'd love to be able to do. She didn't even look nervous. I bet she didn't suffer from anxiety.

Oh, to be like her.

X-treme, X-treme, X-treme, Team Go!
All those tricks I want to know.
Up, up, up in the air so high
Your skateboards flip out in the sky.

Chapter Seventeen

4:24 p.m.

At the end of the show, an older guy, Terry, spoke into the microphone. 'We will be holding a skateboarding clinic over three Saturdays, starting the sixteenth of May, at the Pinnaroo Skate Park. If you're interested come and get a flyer.' He waved them about.

'I gotta get one,' I told Tilly as I stood up quickly.

I went straight to Terry and asked for the flyer. He gladly obliged. Other kids gathered around. Chatter filled the air. Sarah was nearby so I went over to her.

'Hi Sarah, you're awesome! That 540 was incredible.'

She smiled and looked at the flyer in my hand. 'Thanks. Wow, you know the name of the trick. Do you skateboard?'

'Yeah, I do. I'm nowhere near as good as you. I'm working on my 270 and frontside rock n roll at the moment,' I said.

'Cool. That's awesome! Are you going to the clinic? I'll be coaching.'

'Yes, I want to.' I smiled. Inside I was *so* excited. I *so* hoped I would be allowed to go.

'Great, can't wait to see you there! Sorry, I have to go and help pack up.' She pointed to the guys already starting to dismantle the ramp.

'See ya at the clinic,' I said, then jogged back to Tilly. 'Oh Tilly this is so fantastic! I never thought I would have this opportunity!'

'I hope you can go,' Tilly replied.

At home I found Mum at the kitchen table sorting the mail. I shoved the flyer in her hands.

'What's this?' Mum asked.

'It's the X-treme Team Skateboarding Clinic. Can I go pleaseeee?' I held my breath while Mum studied the flyer.

'What will you be doing?' she asked.

I thought this would be easy... but she was in interrogation mode.

'Basic skills and some tricks.' *I didn't ask Sarah that question but what else would you be doing at a skateboarding clinic???*

'Will you be wearing a helmet?' she asked.

'I already wear a helmet Mum.'

'What about your face? We don't want it getting damaged,' she said.

'Mum, please, I'll be careful!'

'I don't know Issy. I'll have to talk to your father and see what he says.'

I went to my room and gnawed my nails. I tried to do some of my Maths homework but I couldn't concentrate. I ended up looking at the answers in the back of the book.

As soon as I heard the front door open, I rushed out to Dad and shoved the wrinkled flyer into his hands.

'What's this Princess?' he asked.

'It's the X-treme Team Skateboarding Clinic. And I REALLY want to go. Can I pleeeeease?'

I clung onto Dad's arm.

Dad glanced at the flyer.

'Sure Princess,' he said.

'Thank you,' I said, hugging him.

I went back to my room and flopped on my bed. The biggest grin spread across my face. I wondered if Tim was going…

I can't wait! ☺

Chapter Eighteen

Friday, 8 May

5:11 p.m.

This semester in Home Ec we've been cooking. I wouldn't say I'm a master chef, or I'd make it on the Kid's Kitchen TV show, but I'm getting a B grade, which is pretty good. ☺

Fried rice was the recipe for today. The kitchen smelt of bacon, fried eggs and soy sauce as the dishes were prepared. I thought mine was yummy but not as good as the Gold Dragon Chinese restaurant's special fried rice we sometimes ate on a Thursday night. Prawns and fried pork would've made it better.

At clean up time Jodie and Oliver were mucking around having a chopstick fight.

'Touché,' I said as I ducked around them to get to the bin.

A silvery glint on the vinyl floor caught my eye, and I bent down to investigate. It was a charm bracelet – in fact it looked like a Pandora.

Who'd have lost it and not known?

I put the bracelet in my pocket and kept cleaning up.

After class I made for the toilets. I locked myself in a stall and pulled the jewellery out of my pocket. The bracelet had five charms. One said confidence, one said happiness, one said prosperity, one said positivity and the last one had engraved on it Sofia loves Ben. This was Sofia's bracelet. Tilly told me she had a boyfriend called Ben. It must be worth a lot of money. I studied the clasp – yes, it said Pandora. I shoved the bracelet back in my pocket. I'd give it to Tilly after school. She could pass it onto Sofia.

At the sound of the home bell, I strolled to the basketball courts, thinking about my find.

Should I give it to Tilly? Can't I keep it for myself? Sofia has heaps of money, she won't miss it, or if she does, she can just buy another one.

I put my hand in my pocket and felt the roundness of the charms.

By the time I arrived at the basketball courts, I didn't know what to do. I reached into my pocket to take the bracelet out, but it felt as if my hand was superglued to the fabric. When I saw Tilly, I kept it a secret.

Once I got home, I went straight to my bedroom, and locked the door. I emptied my pocket. The silver charms glistened in the light coming through my bedroom window. I undid the clasp and placed it around my wrist. Ah, it was so pretty. My 'finders keepers' brain kicked in…

If I take the engraved charm off it, the bracelet can be mine. Sofia doesn't know I found it… nobody does… When am I ever going to get a piece of jewellery worth that much money?

Sparkle, shine, diamond bright.
Flashing flickering in the light.
Come to me you beautiful thing.
In a necklace, bracelet or a ring.

Monday, 11 May

5:17 p.m.

I didn't tell anyone over the weekend about my secret. I wore the bracelet in my bedroom, but not out of it.

If observant Mum saw it, I would be put in the interrogation cell. That would mean another lie. After the hair fiasco I had to be careful.

Last night I tossed and turned. I kept asking myself; *What am I going to do with the bracelet?*

I knew in my heart that I should take the bracelet to school, and give it to Sofia... but I really wanted to keep it.

Can't I do the finders keepers, losers weepers thing? Other people do...

This morning I left the bracelet where it was hidden – in my undies drawer. I departed for school exhausted. My brain = mush.

To add to my predicament, Sofia came up to Tilly and me before school. We were hanging out at the basketball courts. I looked at her distressed face. She was in a panic. I held my breath. *Is she going to say she lost it?*

'I've lost my Pandora bracelet; have either of you seen it?' she asked us.

Yep there it was.

'No Sofia.' Tilly shook her head.

'No,' I answered quickly, staring at the concrete so she couldn't see my face.

'Where'd you lose it?' Tilly asked.

'Don't know. I can't remember where I took it off. Maybe Home Ec. I asked Ms Twain. She sent me to the cleaners but they don't have it.'

'Oh that's awful,' Tilly said.

I looked up to see Tilly drape her arm around Sofia's shoulder. 'I'll ask around.'

'Ben!' Sofia yelled, spotting him. 'Okay, well if you find it or hear of someone having it, tell me.' And off she sprinted.

As I watched Sofia run off. Guilt gnawed at me, like a mouse chewing on a toilet roll. ☹

Chapter Nineteen

Tuesday, 12 May

8:00 a.m.

Ugh I couldn't sleep last night. That guilt I had yesterday never left – in fact in the middle of the night it ballooned. (You could say, the molehill grew to the size of Mt Everest.)

At 2 a.m. this morning, as I lay wide awake, my mind went over all the pros and cons of keeping the bracelet.

The only reason I could think of *for* keeping it was:

1) My parents couldn't afford to buy me one.

But the four reasons *against* keeping it were:

1) It wasn't mine.
2) I would never relax at school.
3) I'd be lying to my best friend who thinks I know nothing about it.

4) And I wouldn't be able to wear it out of my room – what good was that?

So…based on this reasoning I made my decision. I'm not sure how I'm going to give the bracelet back to her, as I don't want to tell Sofia that I found it and wanted to keep it. I will just have to hope God provides the perfect opportunity.

I need to turn this mountain back into a molehill or even smaller, like an ant nest.

5:32 p.m.

God answered my prayer. The perfect opportunity did arise. Sofia has her bracelet back, though less the Ben charm… but that was her choice. ☺

Let me tell you about it.

Walking to school the thought passed through my brain that I could just toss the bracelet into a bush and let someone else find it… I looked around. There were plenty of bushes and trees. I could do that. I took the bracelet out of my pocket. The charms stabbed my clenched palm. I walked on.

I couldn't decide. My brain argued with itself. Beside the creek a garbage truck full of guilt hit me. *You have to give the bracelet to Sofia. Don't throw it away.* I shoved the bracelet back into my pocket and kept going.

When I got to the basketball courts Tilly asked me with concern on her face, 'Are you all right?'

'I didn't sleep well,' I said simply.

The bell rang and we said our, 'See ya laters.' Drinking from the water fountain, I contemplated visiting the school nurse, so I could go home. I swayed... *Yes, no? Yes, no? Yes, no? Ohhh, no.* I decided I should stay. I had an important Science prac in the next period. I trudged to class.

During Science we were studying something on animal adaptations. The prac had been delayed until the next day, Sir said, due to the rats not having been delivered. So I could've gone home. I wasn't concentrating at all, and of course he picked on me for an answer. I had no clue what the question was, so said something I thought might be okay. I can't even remember what my response was. It apparently was stupid because everyone laughed at me, and Sir gave me a stern look. I wanted to crawl under my desk and evaporate. I should've gone home! ☹

Lunchtime arrived and I couldn't hold my secret in any longer.

'I have Sofia's bracelet. I found it in Home Ec last Friday,' I told Tilly.

I could feel my cheeks burning.

'You have Sofia's bracelet and you didn't tell her?' She stared at me for a moment. Her eyes said, 'I'm not impressed.'

'Yes,' I said.

'Geez. Why didn't you tell her?' she demanded. I knew I was in trouble.

'Because I wanted to keep it.' My voice rose in defence of my actions.

'You can't keep it Issy. It's Sofia's bracelet,' she scolded. I felt as if she was smacking me over my knuckles with a ruler.

'Yeah I know. I brought it back today… Can you help me give it back?'

She nodded.

At second break Tilly and I sat together in our usual hang out, talking about the upcoming weekend. Tilly's cousin had her mega twenty-first birthday party. Tilly had a huge family so it was going to be a riot.

'Tilly!'

We looked up to see Sofia, with tears streaming down her face, running towards us.

'What's wrong?' she asked.

'Ben broke up with me,' she sobbed. 'He said he doesn't love me anymore!'

I pulled the bracelet out of my pocket. I hoped she wouldn't ask me how I got it. It wasn't superglued this time. It was time to give it back.

'Sofia is this your bracelet?'

I looked at Sofia's face. It was a mess. She didn't look so pretty after all her crying. In fact she looked rather ugly.

Tilly looked at me and the bracelet. Her eyes said, 'Well done.'

'Yes. Where did you find it?' she asked.

Oh no, I have to think up something quick. 'Um… one of the cleaners gave it to me, and asked me to give it to you.'

'Really? That's awesome!'

Sofia studied the Sofia loves Ben charm on the bracelet and the tears started again. 'I even bought this stupid charm.'

Tilly and I watched as she unfastened the bracelet, removed the charm and threw it at the bin.

'Good shot Sofia.' Tilly said as she landed it. 'You could be a pro-basketballer.'

We all laughed.

I know I did the right thing. ☺

Chapter Twenty

Saturday, 16 May

5:55 p.m.

OMG what a day. Where do I start? We assembled at the skate park at nine o'clock. I counted nine boys, plus myself. The only person I knew was Tim – yes *Tim*! He stood beside me. I could smell his cologne. ☺ The others were both younger, and older, than us. I didn't know if they were all from our school. A couple of the guys glanced at me but nothing else. With my reflective sunnies on, they couldn't see my eyes anyway. I was just part of the boarding crowd. ☺

The X-treme Sports Team introduced themselves: Terry, Mike, Jaycob, Ben and Sarah. The morning began with the basics of skateboarding. After that we were given the opportunity to show a trick we could do – a bit like show and tell. Based on what people demonstrated, they were placed into two groups – the advanced went off with Terry and Mike and the beginners stayed with Jaycob and Ben. I nervously performed a kickflip – something I could do without thinking. (That's what I'd performed for my speech too.) While I was waiting to hear which group I would be in, Sarah came up to me and asked if I'd like to workshop with her. I was stoked. ☺

'That kickflip was really good. What else can you do?' Sarah asked me.

I guess she's forgotten what I told her at school.

'A kickflip obviously… and a backside grind, and a frontside rock n roll. And I'm just beginning to stick a 270,' I told her.

'How about you show me,' she said.

We rolled over to the quarter pipe.

'Show me your frontside rock n roll,' Sarah said.

The butterflies started to flutter and my mind immediately started; *What if I stuff it up? She'll think I'm a liar. Geez.*

I stood on the skateboard, my hands trembling.

'Go,' Sarah said.

I pushed off, but tripped over the board. I blushed.

'Good try. Do it again,' she said.

I pushed off again, but up on the coping lip, stumbled off… just like my first demonstration with Tim.

'I'm not doing it well,' I muttered. 'I nailed it two weeks ago. One of my friends showed me what to do and I've stuck it at the park. I'm just a bit nervous.' I twisted my hands together.

'It's okay. Let me show you, and then we'll go through it step by step.'

I watched Sarah as she executed the trick perfectly. She then worked with me, breaking the trick down into small steps. After a couple of tries, I had mastered it once again. I was putting my foot in the wrong place, like Tim had said.

'You're doing great Issy,' Sarah praised me. 'Can you do the backside rock n roll?'

'I don't know. I've never tried it.'

'All right. It's actually easier than the frontside so I'm sure you'll pick it up really quickly.'

We worked on the trick. She was right – it was easier than the frontside.

'Time for a break,' Sarah told me after we'd both performed the trick.

We rested on the concrete steps, and I pulled out my tuna, cheese and lettuce sandwich from my skateboarder design lunch bag. Sarah had a ham and salad roll. While we ate, we talked. She told me she was nineteen years old. I asked her how she got into boarding.

'I started skateboarding when I was twelve, with my older brother. He was sixteen. He didn't like me tagging along with him, but I didn't care. I ignored his, *Get lost Sarah*s. The gang hung out at the skateboard park, in Springfield, where we lived. I'd watch them, then try and copy the tricks. I had many falls, and broke my arm, and leg, but I was determined. I wanted to be great at boarding. I wanted to stand out. And now I can board better than my brother!' Sarah laughed.

Nathan's face flashed through my mind. *Maybe I should be kinder to him.*

'So how'd you get on the X-treme Team?'

'After I left school I kept practising and getting better. I knew I was getting pretty good when the guys would stop their boarding and watch me. I had respect. One of the guys who went to the skate park often, Jeff, mentioned an audition ad in the local paper, for some of the X-treme Sports. Skateboarding was listed. I sent in my application form and scored a try-out. I was really nervous. My legs were trembling and I thought I would throw up. But I wanted this more than anything. This was my dream.'

'How'd you go?' I so wanted to know.

'I fell off the board to begin with. The guy interviewing me told me to take some deep breaths and centre myself. I did and then tried again. And I nailed it.'

'That's awesome. I always have trouble controlling my nerves,' I admitted.

'I still get nervous before the shows, but I breathe deeply and think positively. I tell myself that it will go well and I'll be fantastic.' She looked so confident.

'I wish I could do that. I get petrified and when I do, I sweat a lot, my heart goes all crazy, and my brain thinks about everything that could go wrong. And then I back out and don't do things. Once I did throw up, I was that scared.'

It felt SO good to tell her.

Sarah nodded. 'I understand completely how you feel. You were a bit nervous for me weren't you?'

'Yeah.'

'Why? Am I scary?' she asked.

'No you're not scary. I thought you'd think I couldn't board after I told you I could.' I stared at the ground.

'You fell off your board. So what? All skateboarders fall off their boards. Even the pros do. I didn't think any less of you. Hey you're the only girl here at the clinic – think about that! You're fantastic for just being here. And you must be here because you want to learn and get better.'

I nodded. 'Yeah I do.'

'I want to help you to improve. I wasn't always as good as I am now. I just have done heaps and heaps of training. Like any athlete you have to put the hard work in to get the results.' Sarah looked at me for a few seconds. 'Something I was taught might help you. It may sound crazy but it worked for me with my anxiety and I think it'll work for you too. Are you ready for my secret?'

I nodded.

'Imagine you're a pineapple.'

'A pineapple?' I asked her.

'Yep, sounds strange I know. But think of a pineapple. It has a thick skin with barbs that are hard to penetrate. If something is thrown at it, it won't split open or leak juice.'

I nodded.

'So now let's relate that to you. If you have a thick invisible skin like a pineapple, you'll be strong and fearless, and you'll keep on trying to get better. You won't care what others think of you failing or stuffing up. It won't matter. You'll know you gave it your best and that'll be all that's important. Everyone makes mistakes. That skin will also stop you from taking on people's negative opinions or hurtful words. What people say will never matter. And if you really want to, you can imagine the spiky leaves are your crown. Be a princess pineapple! And of course being a pineapple, you'll still be sweet on the inside.' Sarah winked at me.

I thought about what she had just said for a while. *A pineapple. Dad would say I'd be a princess pineapple.* ☺

'O-kay.' I was sure I looked surprised.

'Being a pineapple will help you.'

I watched as Sarah fished something out of her pocket. She held it out to me.

'This was given to me by the pro-skateboarder who taught me to be a pineapple. I want you to have it.'

I looked at the silver keyring with the small rubber orange and green pineapple attached to it.

'That's what you need to be,' she said.

I stared at it and said, 'Thanks.'

Chapter Twenty-One

6:25 p.m.

After morning tea we worked on my 270. Once I knew exactly where to put my feet, just like with the other tricks, I mastered the trick. I was stoked. ☺ I still hadn't figured out this pineapple thing though.

'You know what I would really like to do?' I asked Sarah.

'What?'

Maybe she could help me do the thing I'd always wanted to do, but didn't have the guts to do. I told her, 'Go on the half-pipe. I've always been too scared to attempt it.'

'All right let's do it now. You're a pineapple!'

'A pineapple.' I laughed.

Rolling over to the half-pipe I felt on top of the world. All my cares about my face, The Beast, Sofia and Tilly had vanished. I climbed up the ladder with my longboard, and stood on the coping, with Sarah beside me. I followed the ramp with my eyes, down and up to the other side. I imagined myself rolling across, and standing opposite pumping my fists.

My hands immediately started to sweat and my heart thumped. I wiped my hands on my shorts.

'You can do this Issy. Be a pineapple,' Sarah encouraged.

'You do it first,' I said to her, stalling.

'Okay. See you over the other side, Pineapple!' Sarah took off and stood on the other landing. 'Your turn.'

I put my back foot on the board, the front in the air. I faltered.

'Go Pineapple,' Sarah called.

I took a deep breath and took off. Before I knew it, I was up on the coping, beside Sarah. I had blitzed it! ☺

'Yee-haa!' I yelled, fist pumping the air.

Sarah laughed and we high fived. We caught the attention of the guys in the beginners group, who all turned towards us.

Sarah yelled to Jaycob, 'She's facing her fears.'

'Cool,' he called back.

'Do it again,' Sarah said, smiling at me.

Off I went. No nerves. No reluctance. I wobbled but kept going. I was a pineapple!

'Yes!' I fist pumped the air again, over on the coping at the other side.

'You've definitely got potential, Issy,' Sarah complimented me when she had caught up. 'With more practice and hard work, you could one day make the X-treme Team.'

'Really?' I couldn't believe she was saying that.

'Yep.'

The day flew by. I felt bummed when it was over. I had improved so much – I wanted to keep on going. On the upside, there were two more days of the clinic – it wasn't over. ☺ Sarah gave me an X-treme Sports business card with her details on it.

'Email me if you ever want to talk. I'm on Instagram too, and I have a blog – check it out.'

As the team were packing up, I went to chat to Tim. My heart fluttered. I told myself; *Pineapple.*

'How you'd go?' I asked him shyly.

'Great. I nailed my 540. How about you?' he said.

'Awesome. I finally mastered my frontside rock n roll and 270. I learnt how to do the backside rock n roll and I finally went on the half-pipe. It's been so great,' I said smiling.

Tim picked up his skateboard. 'That's cool. Do you want to board some more?'

'Yeah, that would be great,' I said, nodding my head. No way was I going home when I could spend time with him! And The Beast wasn't here to threaten me about it. ☺

We spent the next hour cruising and gliding and rolling. I imagined the skate park as our own private oasis – my Island of Happiness ☺. That deserted tropical island where only Tim and I would live. The poles were palm trees. The concrete area; the sand. The mini ramp; the wavy ocean.

Life was perfect. I couldn't stop smiling and giggling. The time passed way too quickly.

I had to be home by five-thirty as usual. My watch showed five-twenty. If I didn't get home, Mum would be coming to find me, and I didn't want that.

'Sorry Tim, I gotta go,' I told him.

'Okay. See ya later. Will you be here next week?' he said.

I looked at that beautiful face.

'Definitely.' I smiled.

'Great!' He smiled at me and I melted. If I was chocolate I'd be oozing all over the concrete.

Fly to the moon my friend, fly to the moon
Just like the cow who jumped on the spoon
Up the cow zoomed, up like a sword
Up into space on his supersonic board.

Once home I rang Tilly. Of course she was super thrilled for me, wanting to know every small detail. I giggled as I recounted the day to her. When I explained about being a pineapple, she was like, 'What? Hold on, did you say pineapple?'

I told her, 'Yeah a pineapple, you know those orangey-green cylindrical fruits with the thick diamond-patterned skin and spiky leaves.'

'Yeah, I know what a pineapple is,' Tilly retorted. 'Tell me again why you're a pineapple?'

I repeated the analogy.

'Oh okay. That is weird. Just weird,' Tilly said.

'Yeah maybe, but I like it,' I said.

When I got to the part about Tim, and how we spent time afterwards boarding together, Tilly nearly choked on the apple she was eating. ☺

I could hear her spluttering and I giggled.

She asked, 'He asked you to board with him after the class was finished?'

'Yep.' I giggled again.

'Whoa… he likes you Issy!' she squealed.

'You think?' I asked. More giggling.

'Boys don't want to spend time with girls unless they like them. And this is the second time. He's serious,' she said.

By the end of the call my cheeks hurt. After I had recounted my super fantastic day, Tilly expressed that she'd had a boring and angry day, doing chores and fighting with her younger sister. Brianna is eleven and likes to take Tilly's stuff without asking her. At least Nathan doesn't do that – well not yet.

I spent the rest of the night wandering around the house singing. Mum noticed, saying, 'So you had a good time today?'

'Yep, it was awesome Mum,' I told her.

'Any other girls?' she asked.

'No, but Sarah who is one of the team. I told you about her when I gave you the flyer. She workshopped me and she's so *good*. I want to be just like her,' I said.

'Okay.' Mum looked at my shining face. 'Just be careful. We don't want you ending up in hospital.' Her face was serious.

Stop nagging.

'I am, Mum.'

OMG what a fantastic day. I'm riding on clouds. I'm zooming down rainbows. I'm playing in pots of gold. ☺

I still have my rose scented notepaper under my pillow.

Chapter Twenty-Two

Saturday, 23 May

7:20 p.m.

I woke up this morning and smiled. The sun was peeking through my floral curtains. I looked outside at the blue and cloudless sky. Perfect weather for Day Two of the clinic. I ate a huge breakfast of bacon, scrambled eggs and toast, and drank a mug of hot Milo. I hummed while I packed my morning tea and lunch.

'You're happy,' Mum observed again.

'Yep, I love the clinic,' I told her.

'Just be careful please. I don't want a call saying you've hurt your face.'

'I will. Stop nagging me,' I said.

'Isabella, don't be rude.'

Mum has always worried about me injuring my face. When I went roller skating with school, when I learnt to ride my bike, when I told her I played lunchtime t-ball, she expressed her concern. Hmmm. Could that be why she's never watched me board?

Like, I do get why she's so concerned about me boarding. If I told the plastic surgeon what I was doing, he'd probably have a pink fit. So I try to be as careful as I can… but I still want to live a little. ☺

It took me ages to pick out my outfit. I wanted to look nice for Tim. ☺ Not that I had much to choose from. My family doesn't have much money, and bills and food come first. Mum sometimes brings clothes home from the Neighbourhood Friends Charity Shop she volunteers at, and occasionally I get something new. I'm waiting for Mum to have the money to buy a new pair of sneakers for school. My toes are so squashed.

I decided on my three quarter red cargo pants and Peace Out t-shirt. I tucked the pineapple keyring in my pocket, sprayed myself with some vanilla scented perfume, and put on a smear of pale pink lip gloss. Just a touch. ☺

Tim was already there boarding around when I arrived. He waved and came over to me. ☺ He looked gorgeous, in his navy and grey striped shorts, white t-shirt and grey beanie. My heart flip-flopped.

The day began with the choreographing of the show we'd be doing at school. I'm performing a 270 and Tim's doing his 540. That's exciting but scary, all at the same time. As soon as we were told, my brain started its usual twisted troll thoughts; *What if I fall? What if I muck it up? What if people laugh?*

'Stop Issy!' I whispered under my breath. It was time to chuck that nasty negative troll over the bridge (like in the *Three Billy Goats Gruff*) and pick up my invisible pineapple.

I imagined my pineapple – it was golden and sparkly. I picked it up. It didn't hurt my hands. ☺ Using my magical powers, I teleported myself inside of its empty skin. It grew to fit my size. (Extraordinary, I know.) I was now a pineapple – strong and tough. I could do this. If for some reason I failed to stick the trick, it didn't matter, because I was still strong and tough. If that twisted troll wanted to come back to visit, I would stick him with the pineapple leaves – ouch!

Yesterday Sarah also told me that she hadn't stuck quite a few of her tricks. One time, being in the middle of a Royal performance for the Crown Prince and Crown Princess of Denmark, she misjudged her footing, missed the board and crashed to the floor. The undignified landing fractured her collarbone, and the ambulance carted her off, groaning in pain. Sarah was so embarrassed. I could only imagine how she felt. The royals sent a lovely Get Well card and a bunch of flowers to the hospital. How cool would that have been? In the scheme of life, she told me, it didn't matter. Just her ego was dented. (And her body.) Her attitude is so inspiring.

After the choreography we had a practice of the show. Did the pineapple stick it? YES I DID! ☺ Happy dance. Happy dance. ☺

At morning tea, I relaxed on the park bench, watching some of the advanced guys chilling out, doing their own tricks. They were awesome. Sarah had gone off to do some admin jobs. I ate my cheese and crackers, not noticing that Tim had come up from behind. He sat beside me, and started munching on his chicken and gravy roll. This surprised me so much that I breathed in a cracker crumb. Coughs racked my body as I tried to suck in the air, and I flapped my arms, like a psycho headless chook. Superhero Tim saw my distress and smacked me on my back. He then offered me my water bottle, which I chugged.

'You okay?' His eyebrows were furrowed.

'Yeah, thanks.' I felt so embarrassed!

I made a mental note to not have crackers and cheese again. (At least not in front of hot skater boys.☺)

While I recovered, Tim stood up and acted out some of his stories about learning to board, and how he kept falling off. (Remember I told you he was storytelling funny.) Falling off isn't comical but his mimed recounts were. If you can imagine this; on one occasion Tim was boarding around the edge of his mate Josh's pool in the middle of winter. He misjudged the curve, wobbled, trying not to lose his balance, but in he went. It was freezing and everyone stood laughing at him while he shivered like an icicle. No one helped him climb out or even offered him a towel. Another time, Tim was at the beach jumping from the footpath, onto the sand. He slipped, body planted and got a mouthful. His mates teased him, calling him a sand vampire, so he chased them down to the water's edge, wrestling them in the foamy waves. (You had to see his re-enactment. He was *so* funny.) I giggled so much that my tummy ached.

'Stop! I have a stitch.' I told him. (I didn't really want him to stop but if he continued I feared I'd wet my pants.)

Now, it was the *perfect* day until who should arrive? Yes, *her*. Can you believe it? What was she doing there? What gave her the right? This was my territory… She had probably come to watch Tim… How dare she!.. Witch… She even brought a skateboard – a penny.

Mike and Jaycob were talking about different types of boards, so I kept one eye on The Beast at the obstacle course and one on the talk. She looked like a beginner who had no clue what to do. The wheels on her board kept sticking and she'd stumble off… This meant it was a cheap board. It was hard not to notice as well, that she was continually glancing over in our direction.

As soon as our clinic was finished, like a dog tick, she came over and fibreglassed herself to Tim, asking him if he could teach her how to skateboard. I was right. She clung to his arm, fluttered her mascaraed eyelashes, and pouted her red glossed lips at him. I guess she hypnotised him as he said, 'Yeah sure.'

She whispered to me, 'See you later Fish Face Loser. He's mine.' And she tottered after him, flicking her long golden wavy hair. It shone in the sun like an Egyptian goblet.

I desperately wanted to yell out to Tim, and rat on her about being my bully, but I couldn't. Instead I put my head down, and rolled home. She had placed a shadowy cloud in my sunny day. ☹

Once home I made myself a huge bowl of ice-cream: five scoops and chocolate syrup, marshmallows, crushed nuts and a honeycomb choc bar on top. I ate it while I read Mum's *New Day* magazine.

Those Hollywood actresses didn't seem to have as many problems as I did. ☹

Chapter Twenty-Three

Saturday, 30 May

8:00 p.m.

I woke up this morning to another perfect Saturday for boarding. The sky was blue with a few fluffy white clouds. The weather was warm. Today was the last day. I wished the clinic would go on forever with Tim and Sarah. My mind ricocheted to The Beast.

Will she turn up again? If she does, what will I do?

I was still pondering this situation when I started working with Sarah. I must've worn my worry on my face because she asked, 'Is there something wrong?'

I didn't answer for a minute. I wanted to tell her. I was sick of keeping this secret and Sarah was nineteen after all.

'Yeah, there is,' I conceded.

'What?' she asked me.

'There's a girl who bullies me, and she was here last Saturday afternoon,' I said.

'That chick with the wavy hair?'

She's clued in isn't she?

'Yeah, that's her.' I sighed. 'She's hitting on Tim. He's not my boyfriend but I have the biggest crush on him.'

'Why don't you stand up to her or tell Tim what's going on? He seems like a nice guy. It's obvious he likes you. I can see it in his eyes.' She stared into my face, her eyes showing she cared.

'You really think so?'

'Yeah, I can tell these things,' she said, winking at me. I felt my face grow hot.

I looked over at Tim standing with the other advanced guys, working on some air and grab tricks. His longboard leant up against his leg. My heart skipped a beat.

Sarah followed my gaze. 'Do you want me to tell him?'

'Ahhh no. It's all right.' I shook my head.

'I don't think this thing with that girl will last long. He's into his boarding. He'll see through her soon enough. Just be patient. What does she do to you?'

I explained the name calling and pushing.

Sarah was unimpressed. 'That's not good Issy. You need to stand up to her. What do you do when she bullies you?'

'Nothing. I just walk away. When I was little I was taught to say, 'Stop it. I don't like it,' but I can't even say that now.

I'm scared to make things worse.' I told Sarah about the rumour about the knife.

'If ignoring isn't working, you need to stand up to her. You need to be a pineapple with her, just like you're a pineapple for your nerves. It isn't going to stop otherwise.' Sarah stood up. 'And you don't know for sure about the knife – it's just a rumour – it's probably not even true. Come on get up. I'm Tia. Show me what you do.'

I didn't move. I felt stupid, right there in the skate park, acting out the bullying.

'Really now? Here?' I thought she was joking.

'Yep, right now, right here. Get up and let's do it,' she instructed.

I dragged myself up to my feet.

'Come on Issy, you *can* beat her. She's not going to bully you any longer. You are a pineapple,' she encouraged me.

I laughed. 'Yes, I'm a pineapple!' For some reason it sounded really funny. And I laughed so hard, that I collapsed to the ground. My belly hurt.

Sarah pulled me up. 'Come on Pineapple, you can spike her.'

We fist pumped. 'I *will*,' I declared.

'Okay, what will you say to her next time she's mean to you?' Sarah encouraged.

'Um… stop it.'

'You sound like a worm, not a pineapple. Say it like you mean it…. Hey Fish Face what's wrong with your eyes?'

That stung, but out of my mouth came, 'Thanks sweetie pie. They're all the better to see you with.' I had no idea where that rebuttal came from. I preened my hair and strutted like a model.

Sarah laughed. 'Good; that's a start! Sorry for calling you that.'

'It's okay,' I said.

For the next little while we role played what I could say to The Beast so I sounded strong and confident. I must admit it felt good to stand up for myself. I didn't feel like a weak spineless victim. I just hoped I could stand up for myself when I needed to. ☺

Half an hour before the end of clinic, who should arrive on the scene? Yes, *her*. It was déjà vu. I kicked a random stone. I looked at Tim. He hadn't noticed her arrival.

To conclude the clinic, we received *X-treme Sports* bags of goodies: a poster, cap, water bottle, book and stickers. I stuck the cap on. It fitted perfectly. ☺ Next week's school performance was discussed and everyone said their goodbyes. As people dispersed, The Beast moved in on Tim, hanging off his arm. Sarah noticed and rolled her eyes at me. I giggled.

I stood trying to figure out what to do.

Should I confront her here? Could I confront her here?

I knew Sarah would stand with me. My heart began to thump loudly and my hands were sweaty.

No, I'm not ready. Maybe I'm still a worm after all. ☹

146

I rolled off home. My head started beating me up. I had the chance to address my problem, but I wimped out. I should've stood up to her with Sarah, but it was too late now.

When I got home Mum said, 'You're home early.'

'Yeah,' I said, sulking off to my room.

I rang Tilly. I knew she'd cheer me up with something funny. Tilly's solution was, 'You should've tripped her over. That would've got her off the scene.'

I giggled. That's what I needed to hear.

'He likes you, not her,' Tilly told me sympathetically. 'She'll be kicked to the kerb soon.'

'I'm not so sure about that. He's teaching her how to board. He must like her.'

'He's a guy, and she's a pretty girl falling all over him.'

'True.'

I thought about that more after I hung up. I wasn't pretty and I didn't 'fall' all over guys. I never wanted to be a girl like that. My nana always told me, 'Be the apple at the top of the tree that the boy has to climb up to get, not one of the loose ones that are lying on the ground.' ☺

How am I going to solve this problem?

Chapter Twenty-Four

Monday, 1 June

3:34 p.m.

What am I going to do? I have to do an English assignment with THE BEAST. I HAVE NO CHOICE. I even tried to get out of it, but Miss O'Keefe said, 'No swapping.'

Now I must tell you that my horror English lesson began this morning with Miss instructing me, 'Issy, please hand out the novels.'

No drama,

I've done this before. (Miss knows I like helping her.) So I got up, picked up the pile of *Graffiti Suns*, the book we were studying, off the bookshelf at the side of the room, and walked around plopping them on desks. The dog-eared novels had lost their new smell a long time ago. A few groans and mumbles radiated from the back of the room.

The Beast hit me with, 'Thanks Googly Pop.' I ignored her. Now wasn't the time to be a pineapple.

'Okay, who can tell us what has happened in the story so far?' Miss asked, scanning the room.

I looked around. Eyes diverted from her gaze.

She asked, 'Tony?'

'Dunno,' he said.

'I don't know Miss,' she corrected him.

'I don't know Miss!' Sarcasm dripped from Tony's lips. Emily?'

'Um, Lisa was looking for the guy who was graffiti-ing the subway?' she said.

'Yes. Very good Emily. Can anyone else tell me more?'

No hands went up. Miss looked at me. I raised my hand. She smiled. 'Yes Issy.'

I looked directly at her.

'Lisa was walking through the New York subway. She had seen the artwork and the tags and liked them. She decided to go back that night to find out who the artist was. When she was in the subway tunnel a train came and she was pinned up against the wall. She thought she was going to die. She then saw a shadow of a person coming her way... and we don't know who that is yet.'

'That's right Issy!' Miss said half-smiling at me. She gave a deflated balloon sigh. 'I'm glad someone is taking notice of what's happening in the novel! Anybody else want to add anything to Issy's recount?'

There was silence. If you'd dropped a pin, you'd have heard it hit the carpet. Another sigh escaped from Miss's apricot-lipsticked lips.

'Issy can you please start reading from page one hundred and one?' she asked me.

'Sure,' I answered.

I studied her weary-looking face. She must've had a bad day. She wasn't usually like this. Normally, even if no one answered, Miss would be enthusiastic, even pick on one of the jerky guys goofing off in the back row – but not today. I wondered what was wrong. I watched her sit heavily down on the edge of her desk and rub her forehead.

I began to read out loud... 'The shadow came closer and closer as Lisa hid behind the large concrete pole. She could hear a train's horn in the distance...' I read with as much expression as I could.

'Issy I want to stop you there,' she told me.

I focussed on her.

Miss addressed the class. 'Before we continue any further with the novel, I want to ask you a question: Is graffiti art or visual pollution?' She turned to the whiteboard and wrote it in her neat curly handwriting. I heard some, 'What?'s from the back of the room. I turned towards their response, and saw those sweaty smelling guys in the back row staring at Miss. She had their attention now.

'Now stand up,' she directed.

There was a wave of shuffling as chairs moved. Many of the kids were looking at each other, shrugging their shoulders.

'If you think graffiti is art stand near the windows, if you think graffiti is visual pollution, go and stand near the bookshelf.'

What do I think?

I'd never thought about it before. Some of it might be considered art, but what about the majority? A memory suddenly flashed through my mind, making me recoil. When I was five years old, my family went to see the circus in the city park, and I needed to go to the toilets. The public toilets were full of graffiti and they stank really badly. The disgusting sight and smell gave me nightmares for many months afterwards… And there's plenty of ugly tags on buildings, on fences, at the railway… all around Pinnaroo.

An easy decision.

I walked to the bookshelf. No one else joined me. The rest of the class was at the windows.

Miss regarded me and then the window warmers. She said, 'At least we have one person who can think for herself.'

I watched, horrified, as The Beast, wandered across the room and stood beside me. *OH NO.* I looked at the carpet so she couldn't make eye contact with me. She didn't say anything.

Chapter Twenty-Five

3:45 p.m.

We all stood where we were, waiting for Miss O'Keefe's next instruction, 'Okay, back to your desks.'

There was more shuffling of chairs on carpet, and voices saying, 'Why did we do that for?'

Miss presented us with her Chinese torture assignment. 'What I want you to do now, in pairs, is to write a speech to convince your opponents that your opinion is right, and they are wrong. You must persuade them and me. So, Issy and Tia obviously you are together, and the graffiti is art people, you will have to make your own pairs.' There were names being called out and hands being outstretched.

My skin went cold.

What did Miss just say? I have to work with THE BEAST? No, no, no I can't do that. No way.

The blood drained out of my face. If I fainted I could get out of this.

'You will present this to the class Thursday of next week. You can use the rest of this lesson to start work on it,' Miss added.

I raised my hand.

'Yes Issy?' Miss said.

'Can I have another partner? Pleeeeease.' I used my puppy eyes.

'No, sorry Issy. You have to work with Tia.'

My life is over. How am I going to do this?

I dropped my head on the desk, making a loud bang. The Beast snickered at me as she ambled over.

'Oh isn't this going to be fun Puggy,' she snarled in a whisper.

'Miss, can I go to the toilet please?'

She sighed at me. 'No Issy, it's nearly the end of the lesson. You can wait.'

Doesn't she see the panic on my face?

'So, what do you want to do Puggy?' Tia questioned. 'You're the brainiac.'

I looked at the letter P with the spiky crown on top that I had drawn in marker on the underside of my wrist.

You're a pineapple Issy. Prickly, spiky, tough. (But sweet on the inside. ☺) You can do it!

The time had come to address this. I should've done it at the skate park and I hadn't. Now here was another chance.

Did God organise this?

I didn't have anyone standing beside me, but there was a classroom full of people behind me. If she retaliated I would tell Miss, who milled around the room. It was *time*.

Since my bully talk with Sarah, I had been practising what I could say. I had rehearsed a variety of phrases at my reflection in the mirror. I looked The Beast squarely in the face. My heart boomed, and I sucked in the air to steady myself. My hands were sweaty. I held them together tightly on my lap. PINEAPPLE. Here goes… 'What do I want to do? I'll tell you. Stop calling me names. I'm sick of it Tia. My name is Issy. And if you don't stop I'm going to report you.'

The smile faded from The Beast's face, like she had been slapped in the face with a slimy catfish. She sat there staring at me for a minute.

Finally she coughed and said, 'I was just putting you in your place 'cause you're such a snob.'

'What?'

Fortunately, at that exact moment, the bell rang for lunch. I got out of there as fast as I could!

Me, a snob? Am I a snob?

Yay, I stood up to her! Happy dance. ☺

Chapter Twenty-Six

Tuesday, 2 June

7:47 a.m.

Last night I had a really bizarre dream about The Beast. I dreamt that I was an actual alive pineapple with arms and legs, and a funky pair of purple, blue and white sunnies. The Beast called me names and in retaliation, I kicked her up into the outer reaches of the solar system. (Yeah it was a ginormous kick.) To my joy, she was never heard of again, and my pineapple friends and I all held a massive party. ☺ (Maybe the dream was awesome not bizarre.) Shame I can't really kick her up into space...

To be honest, I'm still sceptical about her. Does a leopard change its spots? Until I hear her call me Issy, nicely, more than once, maybe even fifty times, I will be on edge. I don't trust her.

Well, I guess these are the options for this assignment:

A) I don't do it and get an E...
B) I do it all by myself...
C) I leave town...
D) I suck it up and do it with The Beast...

I've thought about the consequences for each. They are:

A) Mum and Dad will be angry, and want to know what's going on. I'd probably be grounded for life!
B) When we do our presentation, and The Beast does nothing, Miss will figure out that I did it all, and I'll get into trouble for not cooperating. That's not good.
C) Where would I go?
D) It will be done and we may even get a good mark. ☺

Well I can't leave town and I don't want to fail, so I *have* to work with her. I keep replaying yesterday's conversation over and over in my mind. *Me, a snob?* I've never thought of myself as a snob. I'm studious and well behaved - not a snob. How unfair!

There's no English today. Yay – I don't have to talk to her... But this afternoon we're meeting at the shops to take photographs of the graffiti around town. We'll see what

she says then. I have to remember that I'm a PINEAPPLE!
Hands; stop sweating.

5:10 p.m.

We planned to meet at the shopping centre, outside
Woolies, at four o'clock. We would then go around
Pinnaroo and take photographs. I was five minutes early.
I stood waiting, my tummy knotting itself. I still didn't
trust her. Her nastiness rattled my brain. I didn't want to
talk to her or spend time with her. To be honest, I still
wanted to cut her up into miniscule pieces.

I hoped to send her to other parts of the town to take
photos. She had a phone, she could do that.

The Beast arrived at four-oh-ten. I mumbled, 'Hi.'

She said, 'Hi,' back, pleasantly.

I wasn't going to be buddy friendly. In my military
voice, I gave her the instructions for where we were going
individually. She told me that her phone was flat so she
hadn't brought it. That meant we had to do it together. ☹

Ugh. Sucky.

We walked to our first spot, the large drain behind the centre. She made small talk. I gave her my 'you've got to be joking' look and ignored her. (You see I can do looks, I'm just not good at comebacks.)

'Okay, so you're not talking to me,' she said. *Yay she's got the message.*

But there *was* one question I really wanted to know the answer to. I blurted it out, 'Why were you expelled from your old school?'

'Um, for wagging it,' she said.

'Wagging it?'

'Yeah, I didn't go to school for a term and they expelled me.'

'You didn't attack someone with a knife?'

'Nope.' That was a simple answer.

How do I know if she's telling the truth?

I studied her face, as I had done when I'd first met Sofia.

'Is that why people have been treating me the way they have?' she asked me.

'How's that?'

'I've had people threaten to stab me.'

'What?' I had no idea.

'Yep.' She stopped walking.

I didn't say any more. Tilly would call that *karma*. I kept on walking towards our next stop, the wall behind the train station. The quicker the better.

'Issy, wait up.' I didn't. She jogged up beside me. 'I'm sorry I've been mean to you.'

Am I actually hearing this?

I didn't reply.

'You're actually an awesome person, and what you said in your speech got to me. I can't imagine having twelve operations.' She sounded genuine.

Should I believe that? Is she just saying it as part of her bait to reel me in?

I clicked away at the messy spray painted tags.

'You can go,' I told her between clicks. I didn't take my eyes off the names on the wall; Casper, TNT, Ark.

'Okay, see you at school.' And she left. I breathed out a large sigh.

Now I'm wondering; *Was she telling me the truth? Has she finished bullying me? Was it that easy to make her stop? Was that true that she got expelled for wagging it? How do I know?* I need a lie detector!

Chapter Twenty-Six

Wednesday, 3 June

3:38 p.m.

In English today, we continued working on our graffiti presentations. I don't understand it, but The Beast was quite nice to me. She did heaps of work editing the slideshow and while we worked she made jokes about the tags I had photographed. It was like working with an alien, or a clone, or something that had its heart swapped. Bizarre, truly bizarre. This whole thing has confused me totally and utterly. Do I put my guard down or do I keep it up? How long does it take to know if someone has changed their attitude? We're hoping for an A grade for our presentation; is that why she's being the way she is?

9:30 p.m.

Tomorrow is the school X-treme Team performance. I'm so excited but *so* nervous.

Be a pineapple: Tough exterior, sweet on the inside. Courage over fear. Believe in myself.

The old questions are penetrating my thoughts, but I'm pushing them away like a bulldozer pushes dirt. ☺

As long as I don't fall, everything will be fine.

Chapter Twenty-Seven

Thursday, 4 June

2:00 p.m.

Well here I am… in hospital. Yep I broke my body. How? Well, things started well then changed quickly.

Standing up in front of everyone was both scary and exciting, all mixed up like a chocolate chip cookie. There were *so* many kids – like most of the school – sitting on the grass watching us. Terry from the X-treme Team gave us an awesome introduction. Everyone clapped and whistled. At my turn I waved and smiled. I heard Tilly's really loud wolf whistle and 'Go Issy!' I felt my cheeks redden and I grinned at her.

The first performance was from the beginners. They did their cross over backside grinds, tic-tacs and ollies. The crowd clapped and cheered. Jarrod stumbled but people whistled even louder to encourage him. He nailed it the second time and took a bow. Everyone in the audience went loony.

Then it was our turn – the advanced group. I was first with my 270. I stood at the top of the coping, my hands sweating and my heart pounding in my ears. My brain yelled, *You're pineapple crush*, but I wasn't going to listen to it this time. I shoved that thought away. I was a strong spiky tough pineapple. I sucked the air down into my lungs. I had practised and practised and practised my trick so I would stick it in the show. I wanted my body to execute it automatically because I knew I would still have some nerves.

I pushed off the coping and rolled up to the other side. The ramp felt different being wooden, and I quickly realised that I didn't have enough air to make the trick. I tried to cut the spin short, but as I panicked I misplaced my front foot. Down I went, crashing to the ramp. I stuck my hand out to stop my face or head from smacking the floor. I heard a crack. The screaming pain radiated up my right arm and I sucked back the tears.

I heard the 'Oooo' from the crowd and Tilly scream, 'ISSY!'

I slumped on the ramp, dazed. Sarah helped me up, and shuffled me to a chair.

She looked at my arm. It was swelling. 'Ring an ambulance,' she directed Mike.

The Deputy Principal, Miss Jones, was quickly beside me. Tilly was too. Someone brought an ice pack to put on my arm. I peeped to see who it was – Tim. ☺

The ambulance arrived and everyone watched as I reclined on the stretcher. Miss Jones, Tilly, Tim and Sarah stayed until the paramedic closed the back door. Tilly was crying. I might've enjoyed all the attention except my arm was in agony. The school had rung Mum. She was on her way. I knew she wasn't going to be happy.

As we left, I saw Mum's car come flying into the school grounds, bouncing over the speed bumps. Miss Jones would fill her in on my injury and where I was going. I hoped Mum wasn't freaking out because if she was, she wouldn't allow me to skateboard anymore. I didn't want that. My life would be over if I was banned from my passion. ☹

Dear God, keep her calm.

Simon the paramedic, in the back with me, took my blood pressure and monitored my sanity. He tried to make jokes, but they were pretty lame. He asked me about my eyes, and I explained to him that I had Crouzons, which he hadn't heard of. That was quite normal – most people hadn't. Simon gave me a whistle with pain medicine in it to suck on. I quickly felt loopy and didn't remember much of the ride.

'We're here,' Simon suddenly announced. The back door opened.

I looked around as I was wheeled into the Emergency Room. The paramedics spoke to a nurse who directed me into a cubicle. There were green curtains, machines, nurses buzzing around, and other patients. I had never been in Emergency before. It was similar to being in the ward, apart from the cubicles which were individual, much smaller in size, and there were curtains instead of walls…

Mum arrived, her face was pale. 'Are you okay Issy? Did you hit your head?'

'No Mum. I put my arm out to save myself,' I told her.

After an hour's wait, which seemed like ten hours, the x-ray people arrived at my bed. The nurse and Mum scattered, and the call of, 'X-ray,' filled the ER. I lay deathly still and waited for the buzz of the machine. We then prepared for the results. Mum sat twiddling her thumbs and rubbing her forehead. I watched the procession of efficient nurses, stern doctors and sick patients.

One of the doctors eventually arrived and addressed Mum. 'Mrs Burgess?'

'Yes,' she answered.

'The x-ray showed she has a fracture of the radius.' He snapped the x-ray on the light up x-ray screen. I don't know what that thing is called. You could see the break. The doctor pointed to the separated bones. 'She is going to need some plates and screws. We'll send her up to the ward and she'll be operated on tomorrow.'

'Thanks Doctor,' Mum mumbled, pursing her lips.

The nurse proceeded to strap my arm in a sling. It ached as she moved it.

'Ow!' I whispered.

'Sorry. You can have some more pain medicine soon,' the nurse commiserated. 'What were you doing?'

'I was performing a skateboard trick, in a show at school, and I fell.'

'Really? A show? You must be pretty good. My son likes to skateboard. He's broken his ankle and collarbone.'

Not sure if she should've said that, as Mum's look could've killed her.

'I love it,' I told the nurse.

Mum went to the Admissions desk. I wanted to ring Tilly, but my phone was in my bag at school. I waited impatiently for Mum to come back.

'Mum, can you ring Tilly's mum and ask her if Tilly picked up my bag.'

'I've got your bag. Tilly gave it to me,' Mum said. 'It's in the car.'

'Oh good. Can you get it for me? I need my phone.'

Mum went to retrieve my bag.

I rang Tilly. She was glad to hear my voice. Her mum would bring her tomorrow to see me. I wish I hadn't fallen. ☹

*

Broken bones hurt so much
Broken bones sore to touch.
Pain – ouchy, ouch, oo.
My poor arm is black and blue.

*

Is this the end of my skateboarding dream?

Chapter Twenty-Eight

5:04 p.m.

I'M upstairs in the ward now. I got here about four o'clock. It's definitely for fractures as there's plaster on arms, legs, and ankles in all directions! There're two other girls in my room. One is a teenager who has a broken leg. I heard her tell the nurse she fell off her horse. Then there's a little girl – maybe four or five. She's so cute. She's got a bandage around her head. Her mum explained to the nurse that she fell off the trampoline (she was doing a somersault) and landed on her head. Ouch.

I've been replaying the accident in my mind, and I'm so embarrassed that I hurt myself, in front of everyone. It was meant to be my shining moment!

Since being here in the ward Mum has been fussing over me. She has kept asking me if I need something to drink, or if I'd like some chocolate, or fruit, or a magazine. I asked for a packet of Malteasers and a *Go Girl* magazine.

I think she was buttering me up because while I was happily sucking the chocolate off the Malteaser ball, and flipping through the mag, in my own little world, Mum suddenly interrupted me and started.

'Issy, there will be no more skateboarding.'

My heart skipped a beat.

Oh no, that's exactly what I was worried about.

I looked up from the mag and frowned at her.

'Don't look at me like that,' she said. 'It's too dangerous. What if you had landed on your face?'

'But Mum I *was* careful. I didn't land on my face. I put my hand out,' I told her.

Her reply was, 'Your father will agree with this Issy. No more skateboarding.'

I sighed. I really wanted to yell at her, about it being my only sense of freedom, and how much she was taking my love in life away from me... But I just kept quiet. There was no point at this moment in making a scene. I would have to work on Dad later.

But I did pipe up with, 'Mum you don't even know what tricks I can do.'

She threw me her, 'that's enough' look.

Tomorrow is my op. ☹

Friday, 5 June

8:50 a.m.

I've just had my calm down pill for my op. I'm feeling a bit spaced out and my hands are shaky.

God watch over me.

11:15 a.m.

The doctor said the op went well. My cast is heavy. My arm's sore. I'm sleepy.

Why did this have to happen to me?

2:45 p.m.

Captain Starlight just dropped in to say, 'Hi'. Captain Starlight's a purple and yellow superhero, with a silver cape, who visits the wards, to make sick kids feel happier. There's more than one Captain Starlight and they all have their own names. The Captain Starlights live in the Starlight Express Room in the hospital, where they have video games and craft stuff that you can do. Captain Starlight and I had a chat and he told me about his skateboarding accidents. No broken bones but plenty of skinned knees and elbows.

'That's why you wear pads,' I laughed at him.

Captain Starlight shook his head at me, and twisted a yellow and green balloon together, making a cool flower, which he kindly attached to the foot of my bed. The Red Cross dropped off some magazines and books. In *Who Weekly* there was an article on Hollywood celebrities who've had plastic surgery to change their looks and to make them look younger – why would they do that? Those women all looked beautiful before the surgeries. Geez, if I looked like them, I'd be so happy. I bet they never got called Fish Face! I showed Mum. She just shook her head.

*

Chapter Twenty-Eight

Doctors come, nurses in tow,
The time in here it goes so slow.
My arm is plastered up to my armpit
An empty canvas – I'll be a hit!

6:12 p.m.

I have news for you tonight. Guess who came to visit me after Captain Starlight? Yep Tilly did, and her mum, but I had some other surprise visitors too. ☺

Tilly arrived with a, 'Hi Issy.' I looked up from my mag to see her coming through the door. My eyes nearly popped out of my head when I saw the people trailing behind her – Tim and Tia. OMG. Tilly's mum brought up the rear. 'Look who I found in the car park,' Tilly said to me. She smiled with her 'surprised' face. Whoa, I was shocked.

'Hi,' I said, surprised too.

'Hi,' they answered together.

Tim's hair was combed back and he wore a nice pair of grey checked walk shorts and a black polo shirt. I could smell that same cologne he wore at the skate park. My heart flip-flopped.

I thought about what I was wearing. My cow print pjs. *Are they stained?*

I looked at them quickly – they were okay thank goodness. I touched my hair… *Oh no, it's probably a mess. Geez, couldn't he have come when I looked prettier?*

Tia coughed. I looked at her.

Why is she here? Is she here because Tim is? Is she concerned about me? Has she changed her spots? How did she get here? Did she come with Tim? Is she with Tim?

Tilly said hi to Mum. Mum then looked from the other two visitors to me, expecting an introduction.

'Mum this is Tim and Tia,' I said, trying to sound calm and not give away my super crush.

'Hi,' they both said.

'Here, I have a pressie for you.' Tilly said interrupting us, handing me a gift bag. I excitedly looked inside. I pulled out a fluffy brown teddy bear that was wearing a blue bowtie and had a bandaged arm.

'Aw, he has a broken arm too. Thank you, he's so cute and soft.' I hugged the bear then asked Tilly to tuck it under the crisp white sheets beside me.

'Sofia wanted to come, but she wasn't allowed. She gave me this, to give to you,' Tilly told me, handing me a small Get Well Soon gift bag.

'Really? That's so nice,' I said, feeling shocked. She didn't even know me, and I made her leave Tilly and me... Inside the bag was a pretty blue jewellery box. In the box was a silver chain with an infinity pendant.

'Oh, it's beautiful,' I squealed. 'Tell her I said thanks. Can you put it on me?'

Tilly looked at me with her 'how does it feel to be given two gifts by your friends?' look as she fastened it around my neck. I now understood how she felt about her birthday gifts.

'So I'm still your best friend?' she joked.

'Yes!' I exclaimed, blushing. 'Sorry.' Nothing more was said. Nothing more needed to be said. We both knew what the sorry was for.

Tim interrupted, giving me a pretty bunch of flowers. There were pink carnations and white lilies and baby's breath. I blushed and said to him, 'Thanks.' I studied the flowers as I tried to hide my cheeks, which for sure were hot red by now. Tia interrupted my camouflage attempt, by shoving a present at my head. I unwrapped it – a green and silver striped journal. I muttered and half-smiled, confused about why she was here. 'Thanks.'

Chapter Twenty-Nine

6:59 p.m.

Tilly's mum, Mrs Watkins, who sat on a chair beside Mum, asked me, 'How are you Issy?'

I told her, 'My arm hurts a bit. They put plates and screws in it.'

She gave me a sympathetic smile.

'Can we sign your cast?' Tilly wanted to know.

'Sure,' I told her. 'I think there's a pen in the drawer.'

I watched as Tilly found the pen, then drew a Peace sign and wrote, 'Get well soon bestie! Love Tilly xxx' on my cast. Tim wrote, 'Get well soon. Tim ☺.' I didn't want Tia to write anything but how could I say no? She wrote, 'Tough chick. Tia'.

Mrs Watkins and Mum went out to the play area to have a chat.

We spent the next half an hour, talking about my accident, and how it had spread all around school. Everyone knew Issy Burgess had fallen off her skateboard in the show. An uncomfortable lump formed in my tummy.

How can I go back to school?

Tilly's mum came back into the room and told me, 'Sorry Issy, but we have to go. I have to pick up Tilly's father at four o'clock.'

They said their goodbyes and left.

'My dad's in the car waiting,' Tim said. 'So we have to go too.'

Huh, so that means he and Tia came together? How confusing. They said, 'Goodbye,' too.

Mum settled in the chair beside me and worked on another one of her crosswords. I closed my eyes and pictures of Tim and Tia flashed around, morphing into a two-headed monster. I drifted off into a weird dreamland.

'Issy?' a voice intruded my floating subconscious.

I opened my eyes.

'Sarah?' I didn't expect to see her.

'Hey. How are you?' She sat on my bed.

'Sore. I've had plates and screws put in my arm. I did it well. I'm a smashed pineapple,' I told her.

Sarah laughed. 'Yep, that you are.' There was silence. 'But you tried, Issy.'

'Yep. But now Mum says I can't board anymore.' Mum wasn't in the room so there wouldn't be an argument.

'She'll come around. She's just being protective of you. My parents were worried when I joined the X-treme Team.

They wanted me to stop when I fell at the Royal Show. I didn't stop though. It's in my blood. I have to board.'

I felt like a younger version of Sarah. I said, 'That's how I feel. I feel so free when I board. All the stuff I worry about just goes away.'

Sarah nodded at me, saying, 'I have something for you. I hope you like it.'

She handed me a present, the size of a piece of photocopy paper, but a lot thicker. *What is it?* I untied the white ribbon, and unwrapped the neat rainbow spotted paper. I opened the flaps of the plain black box that was inside. I pulled out a wooden frame and studied the picture. It was a pineapple. At the bottom, under the pineapple, a quote said, 'You become what you believe'.

'I painted it,' Sarah told me smiling.

'I love it. You can paint too?'

'Yeah; not as well as I board.' Sarah laughed.

'It's great. I like to draw,' I told her.

'Really? What do you draw?'

'Mainly Anime characters. I don't have my sketchpad, otherwise I'd show you some.'

'That's cool.'

I put the pineapple picture on the bedside table beside Tim's beautiful bouquet.

'They're pretty. Who are they from?' Sarah asked.

'Tim,' I said, grinning.

'Oh, really?' Sarah's eyes lit up and twinkled.

Chapter Twenty-Nine

'Yeah, but he came with Tia. I think they're going out…'
I said glumly.

'Doesn't matter if they are. He came to see you and brought
you flowers. He cares for you. It won't be long and he'll see her
true colours. Have you stood up to her yet?' Sarah said.

'Yeah I did, but I still don't trust her. *And…* I even have to
do an English assignment with her. Ugh.' I grimaced. (It felt
good to be able to tell her I had.)

'That's awesome! Well done for standing up to her. I
knew you could do it. Has she stopped?' she asked.

'So far.' I smiled.

'That's good. So how'd you end up with her for your assignment?'

I explained the graffiti project.

'Maybe the universe is testing you, stretching you. There
are no coincidences; everything happens for a reason.'

I looked at Sarah. 'Well I don't like it.'

'You're strong now Issy. You'll cope. Message me with
what happens okay?'

I promised I would, and Sarah said her goodbyes.

I pondered over the 'no coincidences' comment.

Do I believe everything happens for a reason? Do you?

Chapter Thirty

Saturday, 6 June

1:14 p.m.

This morning I came home. Dad hung my pineapple picture on the wall above my bed, and I set the bandaged bear on my quilt, beside my small collection of Beanie Bears. I put my skateboarding bear and the bandaged bear beside each other.

I'm nervous about going back to school.

What if I'm teased or laughed at for falling off my board? Pineapple. I'm a pineapple.

Pineapple, pineapple, yes I am.
Not an apple or a ham.
Thick skin and sweet as can be.
A pineapple, a pineapple that is me!

Monday, 8 June

4:15 p.m.

Going to school today was hard. I wished I was one of those cool cucumber or laissez-faire kids. I was *so* tense. My hands sweated. I stood at the front gate, took a deep breath, wiped my hands on my shorts and walked in. I told myself, '*Pineapple, you can do this.*'

The first group of kids who saw me said, 'Hi Issy, how's your arm?' I didn't even know them.

This continued all day. Kid after kid after kid said, 'Hi Issy' and 'How's your arm?' and 'Does it hurt?' and 'Can I write on your cast?' I didn't know the majority of them but they knew me!

I felt like a rock star or a princess or something. Is this how the Royal Family in England feels? I must admit that I do like this 'being known' thing. ☺ I took a photo of my cast and put it up on Facebook. It's *full* of messages and pictures. (I've already got ten comments and twenty-seven likes. ☺)

*

I thought I'd failed, in fact I'd won.
Breaking my arm wasn't much fun.
Fame awaited me going back to school
I was treated like an expensive jewel.

*

It looks like all that worry was for nothing. ☺ Yay!

Tuesday, 9 June

5:32 p.m.

Ugh. My conclusion about Tim and Tia was right. Today they were holding hands! I really thought Tim was above her. How could I be so wrong? I don't understand it and I'm way jealous. ☹ I hope he'll see her true colours soon, just like Sarah said, and drop her like a hot potato. And if she dares call me a name, I'm going to dob on her. I'll report her to the Year Nine Co-ordinator, and spill what's been happening to me. I'm pretty certain Tim would dump her for that.

After I saw them together, at the next break I had to tell Tilly. She was sad too as she had seen Sam with a girl.

'He's missing out on the best girl,' I told her.

'Yep. Tim is too,' Tilly told me.

'Let's go get some strawberry sorbets,' I suggested. For the rest of the break we sat eating and commiserating with each other. In the love stakes we'd both struck out.

Wednesday, 10 June

7:36 p.m.

Wow, what a day. I'm soaring high on my supersonic board tonight! ☺

Today on Assembly, I was called up to the podium. I had no idea why. Usually we get told if we're getting an award, not that it was award season. All the kids in my class swung to stare at me with wonderment. I noticed Tia kept her gaze on the Principal. Jillian, beside me, nudged me. 'Go Issy!'

As in a weird dream, I rose and walked up the stairs on the side of the stage. There were a few whispers, and I could feel a whole school of eyes boring into me. I stood beside Mr Schulter, our Principal. The lights on the stage were warm. I gazed out over the sea of navy and white uniforms and blank faces. My legs began to shake.

'Students, I have called Isabella up to the stage for an important reason,' Mr Schulter began. I stared at him.

What reason?

'She was the only girl involved in the X-treme Sports Skateboarding Clinic, and I had a wonderful report from the coaches, about her talent and dedication to the sport.'

Has Sarah said something about me?

Mr Schulter pivoted towards me.

'Issy, I have been given this trophy, by the X-treme Team, to present to you. Unfortunately they couldn't make it this morning, as they have a show on at another school, but they will be here later on today, for an interview with the Pinnaroo Press.'

What? Trophy? Pinnaroo Press?

I was trying to take everything in but I was in a bit of a daze. He handed me the trophy and I took it robotically, then smiled while Mrs Ball took a photo.

I went to walk off.

'Don't go Issy…' Mrs Ball said. I stopped.

Mr Schulter continued, 'I would also like to present to you a Certificate of Courage. We here at Pinnaroo are very proud of you. Now I know you still have six weeks or so, with your broken arm, but we are looking forward to hearing how your skateboarding ventures are going, once you have recovered.'

I mumbled, 'Thanks,' grasping it with my plastered hand. The school erupted with applause. My cheeks burned.

More flashes illuminated me.

I walked back down the stairs carefully so as not to stumble or fall. It was all totally surreal. I sat down and Jillian inspected my trophy. I couldn't help but smile. ☺

Wow, I didn't see that coming. Did he really say the Pinnaroo Press is coming?

After lunch the Pinnaroo Press reporters arrived. They told me they were writing an article on the skateboarding program. Sarah and Terry came, both congratulating me on my trophy and certificate. Sarah said to me, 'You truly deserve them Issy. You have heaps of talent and potential.'

'Thanks Sarah.' I couldn't stop smiling.

The photographer took an individual photo of me holding the trophy and certificate, and then there were group shots. Tim was in those. The reporter interviewed me about what it was like being a female skateboarder. I said something like, 'It's cool. I love the freedom and the challenge of learning new tricks. It's a great sport for girls.' They asked me about my broken arm, and I explained how I fractured it during the show, doing one of my tricks. They then questioned me if I still thought it was a great sport for girls after I broke my arm? I told them, 'Yes. You can break your arm doing any type of sport.' They nodded their heads at that. ☺ The other guys were asked about their experiences too, and Sarah, Terry and Mr Schulter talked about the program.

I can't wait to see the paper on Friday. ☺

Chapter Thirty-One

7:50 p.m.

Once I got home this afternoon I went looking for Mum. I heard the vacuum cleaner in her bedroom. She couldn't hear me over the noise. I walked quietly up behind her, and tapped her on the shoulder. She shrieked. I laughed and said, 'Hi Mum.'

Mum put her hand on her chest and panted. 'Oh Issy, you scared me!'

I stood on the 'off' button. Nathan scurried into the room, having heard the scream.

He stared at Mum and me.

'I got something today.' I smiled.

'What?' Mum asked.

'Come out to the kitchen,' I said, turning to leave the bedroom.

They followed me out.

'Ta da!' I waved my arms, plaster and all, at the trophy and certificate sitting on the kitchen table.

Mum picked up the trophy and read the plaque. She then read the certificate. Nathan huddled beside her, scanning them too.

'These are for your skateboarding?' Mum looked at me, confirming what they were for. Her eyebrows looked like they were narrowed – like she wasn't totally happy about what she was reading.

'Yes. The trophy is from the clinic, and the certificate's from school. I had to go up on stage at Assembly to get them.'

Mum's face changed to a smile. It didn't look genuine. A real smile makes her eyes twinkle, and they were dull.

'Wow,' said Nathan. 'That's cool.' He seemed genuinely impressed.

'Thanks.' I grinned at him. 'And I'll be in the paper on Friday. The Pinnaroo Press came to school.'

'Really?' Mum said, raising her eyebrows at me.

'They took photos and interviewed me,' I told her. 'I can't wait to see it,'

Mum was silent.

'Cool,' Nathan said again.

'Don't tell Dad. I want to show these to him,' I told them, picking up the trophy and certificate to take back to my room.

'Okay,' Mum said.

Mum went back to her vacuuming and Nathan sauntered back to watching TV.

I showed my winnings to my hermit crabs. 'What do you think boys? Pretty cool eh?'

Only Rockmiester peeked out from under his shell. I placed my trophy and certificate on my dressing table, then laid on my bed and remembered the day. It was out-of-this-world fantastic!

I eventually heard Dad's voice. I came out of my room and went to find him. He was in the family room chatting to Mum about some client. I interrupted.

'Dad, I've got something to show you.'

Dad's eyebrows raised at me. 'What, Princess?'

'It's a surprise.'

Dad looked to Mum for a clue but she didn't give one.

'Hang on, I'll be right back,' I told him.

I hid my prizes behind my back, then presented them to Dad who'd followed me to my room. He studied the trophy's engraving first.

'It's from the clinic, Dad. The certificate is from school, and I had to go up on stage during Assembly today. Mr Schulter presented them to me.'

Dad read the award then his big arms encircled me. 'That's fantastic!'

'Thanks Dad. And I'll be in the paper on Friday,' I babbled.

'Really, the paper? My Princess is a star.' He kissed the top of my head.

'Yep.' I jumped up and down.

'That's wonderful. I think this deserves a celebration. So what would you like for dinner?' he asked me.

Mum must've had an inkling Dad might say that, as she hadn't started cooking.

'Fish and chips please,' I said.

'All righty, fish and chips it is!' Dad exclaimed.

Mum emerged from doing the ironing, and stood beside Dad. Dad was grinning, but she looked like she'd just sucked on a lemon. (Well lemon does go with fish and chips. ☺)

I smiled at them. If Mum started her, 'You can't skateboard anymore' stuff, I was sure that Dad would stick up for me. ☺

9:52 p.m.

Tomorrow I have my graffiti presentation with Tia. ☹ I've been trying not to think about it but as I've been lying here trying to sleep, my anxiety has started to say hi to me. Maybe she'll be sick so I can do it on my own.

Dear God, Help me to be a pineapple. Take my fear away and give me courage. Amen.

Thursday, 11 June

3:51 p.m.

Give us a G, Give us an R, Give us an A, Give us a FFITI.
What does it spell – GRAFFITI.
Graffiti, graffiti is everywhere.
Graffiti, graffiti it does scare.
Graffiti, graffiti put your spray cans away
Graffiti, graffiti it's art – no way!

Well, I'm glad that's over. Tia wasn't sick… I put on my 'just gotta get through this' pineapple face. I had a few sweats happening. She did her part and I did mine. I didn't talk to her before or after the presentation. We got an A-. I'm stoked. ☺☺

Friday, 12 June

7:00 a.m.

I'm on the front page of the Pinnaroo Press! I woke up an hour ago, rushed outside in my panda pjs and unravelled the paper. Who should be staring back at me on the FRONT PAGE? Yep *me* – the photo of me holding my trophy and certificate. The headline read, 'Issy's born to board'. I skimmed the article, and they'd put in what I'd said. There was more on page six. Flipping to the page, I saw the group photo. How awesome. ☺

I ran back into the house, slamming the front door. 'Mum, Dad, Nathan, I'm on the front page of the paper!' I yelled.

Nathan came out of his room yawning, his hair a bird's nest. Dad came tying his tie, and Mum was in her robe. I laid the paper on the table. They gathered around it, reading the article, turning to page six to read the rest.

'My famous Princess,' Dad said cuddling me.

'They're nice photos,' Mum said. She didn't mention the actual article.

'Can I take it to school?' Nathan asked.

Chapter Thirty-One

'No, I'm taking it to school today. You can take it on Monday,' I told him.

'We can get another couple of copies,' Dad said. 'I want to show the office.'

Woohoo, how awesome is this! ☺

4:08 p.m.

Wow what a day at school. I was a star again! (I like writing that. ☺) So many kids and teachers told me they'd seen the paper. And Tim came to ask me if I'd seen it.

'Yes,' I said. 'It's great.' Happiness bubbled from me. He thought so too.

How good am I?! ☺ Has this changed my life?

Chapter Thirty-Two

Saturday, 13 June

Midday

I went to the skate park this morning, with my cast on. I was careful and stuck to the obstacle course. It actually was a bit tricky with one heavy arm and one light one. I found that I could only use my free arm for balance. But I have to tell you, that it felt *so* good to be back on my board. ☺ Freedom…

Mum and Dad weren't too happy when they saw me with my penny board under my arm. Mum stopped me abruptly after I'd stated, 'I'm going to the skate park.'

In fact her eyes nearly popped out of her head. I wanted to laugh at her face, but I knew what the consequences would be if I did. I stood waiting for what was coming – those eyes meant she wasn't happy.

'Issy, you can't go to the skate park,' Mum said.

'Why? I'll be careful.'

'No Issy. I don't want you to hurt more of yourself.' Mum folded her arms.

'Oh Mum, I promise I will stick to the obstacle course. I won't go near the pipes. I'll be *very* careful.'

Dad walked into the room.

Before Mum could say anything I asked, 'Dad can I go to the skate park pleeeeease?'

'I don't think she should,' Mum said. Her face had that 'just sucked a lemon' look again.

'Pleeeeease Dad. I'll stay on the obstacle course. I'll do nothing else... I promise.' I smiled my sweetest smile.

Dad looked from me to Mum, then back to me. She was shaking her head. I held my breath. It was up to Dad. *Pleeeeease Dad.*

'Do you promise to stay on the flat parts? No pipes or stairs or anything like that,' Dad said.

'Yes Dad.'

I waited. Dad looked at me for a few seconds. I put on my sweetest smile.

'All right, off you go. Be back by midday,' he said.

'Yes I will,' I said grinning. I kissed him on the cheek and said, 'Thank you.' Then I scooted out the door before he changed his mind. As I left I heard Mum grumbling something to him.

Mum is such a worrywart. I know she doesn't want me fracturing my other arm and to be truthful, I don't want to either. That would be sucky. If I had no working arms, who would wash me and take me to the toilet? Mum? *Ew*. No. I like my privacy and independence, thank you very much.

And I have to tell you that I was so glad I went... Tim was at the skate park and on his own. ☺ As soon as he saw me, he came over to where I was. We boarded around the obstacle course together and followed the concrete paths around the park. We chatted and he told jokes, making me laugh. It felt so right to be with him. ☺

The entire time though, I was waiting for him to say something about Tia. He didn't. I wanted to know; Were they still going out? The question sat on the tip of my tongue but when I tried to ask it, it would slip down and become a lump in my throat. I just couldn't do it. I'd have to wait a bit longer to find out. Ugh.

Chapter Thirty-Two

Sunday, 14 June

5:50 p.m.

This afternoon I went boarding again. Tim was there – and alone. I couldn't help but think; *Is he here to see me? Is this a God thing?* ☺

I remembered Sarah saying, 'There's no coincidences.'

This Tia thing was eating me up like a flesh-devouring Piranha. I *had* to know the answer. It didn't look like he was going to tell me if I didn't ask.

I stepped into my invisible pineapple suit, took a deep breath and before the lump could form I asked him, 'What's the go with Tia?'

'We're going out,' he replied.

This three word statement hit me like a bullet to the heart. Yeah I know it was what I suspected but it was hard to hear coming out of his beautiful mouth. I wanted him to say, 'Nothing's going on.'

'Oh,' was all I could mutter.

Tim gave me a strange look but didn't say anything else.

Don't you think he needs a girl who does board – like *me*? ☺ It won't last. You know, I've pressed one of the carnations and lilies from my bouquet he gave me in hospital. ☺ I wonder if he's given her any flowers.

Monday, 15 June

3:47 p.m.

Oh boy she's asking for it! I'm going to get her back. She's still The Beast. You don't mess with a pineapple. I'm not that old wimpy, lay down and take it Issy anymore. I'm shoot it from the hip, or stab you with my barbs Issy.

Let me tell you what went down today. It was the end of lunch and I was coming out of the toilets. The Beast put her hand out and stopped me. There I was, thinking she was going to say something nice to me... and this happened. 'Stay away from Tim, Poppy Eyes!'

I stared straight into her eyeballs. I hadn't noticed before that one of her eyes was smaller than the other... 'What's your problem?' I calmly asked her.

I didn't think she expected that.

'Stay away from my boyfriend, got it?' she said.

'Nope. Not going to happen. You know we both like boarding.' I told her. I was still calm.

She poked me in the chest and strode off. My heart pounded like a sledgehammer and I felt like collapsing to the floor.

What the heck was that all about? She must feel threatened. I smiled to myself. *Cool.* ☺

I rang Tilly when I got home. She let fly a few choice words, I can't repeat. ☺ 'He must be talking about you or she wouldn't have said that to you. He likes you Issy,' she told me. I giggled.

Even though I wanted to daydream about Tim, I knew it was time to tell Tilly the truth about Tia. No longer was I going to be under Tia's control.

'Um, I need to tell you something.'

'What? Sounds serious,' Tilly said.

'Yeah, it is. Tia's been teasing me about my eyes and she's been pushing me around... since last year.' There I had said it.

Tilly wasn't happy. 'What? She's still doing it? I thought she'd stopped because you hadn't said anything.'

'No, she's still going.'

'Why haven't you told me?' Tilly was now angry with me.

'I don't want her threatening me with a knife.' There was the reason, out in the open now.

'Oh Issy! What am I going to do with you?' I could hear the exasperation in her voice.

'Be my best friend,' I said sheepishly.

'Ha ha, yes, but best friends stick up for each other. She's not going to be teasing you any longer. She's in for it,'

Tilly stated. 'And Tim will not want to be with her when I tell him what she's been doing to you!'

'What are you going to do?' I asked.

We spent the next half an hour discussing things we could do. Some of them I must say weren't nice, but they were funny. The final plan had to be non-violent – we didn't want to get suspended.

What Tilly came up with, sounded like it might just work.

Wednesday, 17 June

7:12 a.m.

This morning is D-day. How's it going to go? Will it backfire on us? At least I'm not doing it alone. It's a great plan. Tilly, Sofia, and Alisha (who's Sofia's new friend) are involved. When Tilly asked Sofia yesterday for help, she was in straight away. She then suggested Alisha as well. Alisha is a *really* tall girl. She's tough too. She makes The Beast look like a pussy cat. I'll tell you this afternoon how it goes. What will happen?

Chapter Thirty-Three

3:58 p.m.

Well we did it. I think I'm on my way to being free from my bully. She sure was put in her place. ☺

The plan began with Alisha approaching The Beast after German, and asking her if she wanted to watch the teacher/student volleyball match. The Beast said, 'I'm going with Tim.' We thought that might happen so Alisha told her, 'All right, well, I'll see you there,' and she quickly came back to us.

Tilly, Sofia, Alisha and I stood near the courts, where we could see her and Tim coming.

My heart pounded as they walked towards us. My palms felt like soggy sponges. It was time. We pretended we were chatting.

Alisha and Sofia stopped and stepped towards the duo. Alisha called out, 'Hang on Tia, gotta ask you something.'

The duo stopped.

Alisha asked her, 'What's the deal with you, picking on Issy about her eyes?'

The Beast replied with, 'I haven't done anything to Isabella.'

'Issy, come here,' Sofia called.

I walked over to them. Tilly followed me. It was now the four of us.

Tia stared at me. 'I haven't teased you about your eyes have I?' she asked me, with a 'you better not tattle on me' look on her face.

Pineapple time.

I stared her straight in the face and crossed my arms.

'Yes, you have, and you know it. You've been teasing me about my eyes since you arrived last year.'

I could feel my heart pumping.

'No I haven't. You're lying,' she said.

'No, you're the liar and you'd better stop!' I told her.

'And you better not tease her anymore, Tia, or we'll report you,' Tilly warned.

'Yeah we will,' agreed Sofia and Alisha together.

Tia looked at each of us, then said to Tim, who was standing watching the altercation, 'Let's go.'

We watched as they walked off. I couldn't hear what they were saying.

'Thanks guys,' I said to my friends. They were awesome. ☺

Time would tell whether the plan had worked.

Will she stop teasing me and will Tim leave her?

I'm off to the skate park. Wonder if Tim will be there?

6:00 p.m.

Woohoo, Tim was there. ☺ I felt a bit nervous when I saw him. Would he be nice or mean to me? What if he was angry with me?

Be a pineapple, I told myself.

Tim came over to me. 'What's going on with Tia?' he asked. He seemed calm. His eyes were relaxed. He smelt good. ☺

'She's been calling me names and stuff,' I said simply. 'And it's been going on for a long time. I thought my English speech would stop her, but it hasn't.'

We rolled over to the mini ramp. Tim helped me to climb up to the coping. His hands felt so strong. We sat on the top of the mini ramp with our legs dangling, and talked. Tim wanted to know everything, so I told him. At the end of my recollection his eyes were dull.

'Why didn't you tell anyone?' he asked me.

'I thought she might threaten me with a knife.'

'Why would you think that?'

'That rumour when she arrived.'

'What rumour?'

'That she was expelled from her old school for threatening someone with a knife.'

'I didn't hear that one. She told me it was because she was wagging a lot.'

'I asked her when we did the graffiti assignment and she said the same thing.' I took a deep breath and changed the topic. 'I told Sarah about Tia at the clinic, and Sarah told me to be a pineapple towards her.'

'A what?'

'A pineapple.'

He raised his eyebrows at me.

I chuckled. 'Yeah I know it's strange but yes a pineapple.'

'Okay. What does that mean?'

'Basically have a tough exterior like the barbed thick skin and be sweet inside.'

'Okay. You are sweet inside.'

'Thanks,' I mumbled.

'You're blushing. See; you are sweet.'

I covered my face with my hands for a minute. Tim gently pulled them off.

'Being a pineapple also means, you become what you believe. I believed I couldn't do things, so I didn't do them, like I didn't swim in the carnival, because I thought something bad would happen. And I let Tia bully me, because I was scared of what she might do to me.'

'I didn't swim because I *know* I'm hopeless at it!' Tim laughed. I laughed too. 'And has being a pineapple worked for you?' *He's being so caring.*

'Yep, it calmed me down. Now when I'm freaking out, I put on my invisible pineapple suit which will protect me. I'm also trying to not let my 'things might go wrong' thoughts stop me from doing stuff. Things could go right!'

Is he going to laugh at that? Will he think I'm stupid?

Tim said, 'That's cool.' He didn't laugh.

'She also gave me this.' I pulled my pineapple keyring out of my front pocket and gave it to Tim.

'And Sarah also painted me a picture of a pineapple which says underneath, *You become what you believe.* She gave that to me in hospital. Dad hung it above my bed.'

We were both quiet for a minute. Then Tim said, 'Issy if she *ever* teases you again let me know, and I'll deal with her.'

'Thanks.' I smiled sheepishly.

'How's your arm?'

'It's not as sore as it was. Two weeks to go and the plaster comes off.'

He spent time reading the messages, and commenting on the pictures on my cast. Then we cruised around the obstacle course, and Tim performed some tricks on the mini ramp, while I watched and cheered him on. I even videoed a few of them for him. They're going up on YouTube. I floated home. ☺ Woohoo!

I still don't know if he'll break up with her. He didn't say he was going to. ☹

Chapter Thirty-Four

Sunday, 21 June

1:11 p.m.

I've been doing a lot of thinking about Sofia. She didn't have to buy me a present when I broke my arm. She didn't have to help me with The Beast. She didn't have to ask Alisha to help. She's a nice person. ☺ She must like me, or she wouldn't have done those things. I've been a nasty cow. OMG – have I been a green-faced witch?

I think I need to fix things up. It's not right to keep Tilly to myself. I'm not her keeper. If she wants other people to sit with her, then I should be happy with that. Tomorrow I'm going to tell Tilly that Sofia and Alisha are welcome to sit with us. Or even anyone else, if she wants. Is my halo a bit more sparkly? ☺

Monday, 22 June

3:55 p.m.

I spoke to Tilly this morning about Sofia, and she was stoked.

'That's awesome Issy!' she told me, grinning. 'I'll ask Sofia in English.'

At lunch, Sofia and Alisha arrived at our hangout. We all chatted and laughed, and Alisha told silly stories. It was a good time.

Life is great! ☺

Tuesday, 23 June

4:07 p.m.

Guess what I did today? I stood UP for Sofia! Yep, I was a pineapple. I'm so stoked. ☺

This is what happened…

At first break, Tilly, Alisha and I were drawing some Anime characters. Sofia came rushing over to us. Her thumping shoes made us look up. Her face looked like thunder, and lightning strikes were about to come shooting out from her nose (well, not really ☺).

'What's wrong?' we all asked her together.

'That Shannon just threw my bag in a puddle!' She held up her backpack. The leather was dripping and mud stained. 'It's ruined!'

I gasped. Tilly and Alisha just stared.

'Let's try and wipe it off,' I said, standing up. 'I'll go get some paper towels from the toilets.'

I came back with a handful, and cleaned up her bag, the best I could. It still didn't look too good.

Sofia looked at it, shaking her head. 'She's ruined it!'

'Why'd she do that for?' Alisha asked her.

'She reckons I told her boyfriend some bad stuff about her. I have no clue what she's talking about! I didn't even know she had a boyfriend,' Sofia said.

'What?' Tilly said.

A thought popped into my head.

'Do you think it might be Tia, trying to get back at you, for sticking up for me?' I asked her.

'Oh,' Sofia said. 'Maybe that's it!'

'Let's go find out.' I stood up.

The others followed my lead.

We wandered the school in search of Shannon, finally finding her near the Technology room. She was sitting with her friends, but that didn't stop us.

'Shannon, why'd you throw Sofia's bag in the puddle?' I asked her.

She jerked her head up and glared at me, saying angrily, 'She talked rubbish to my boyfriend about me.'

'No she didn't. She doesn't even know your boyfriend. Who told you she did?' I said, crossing my arms. (I didn't have any anxiety. Woohoo! ☺)

Her group all stopped their eating and stared at me.

'Tia.'

Boom. There it was!

'Well Tia's lying, Shannon. It was probably her. You need to get your facts straight,' I said.

'Do you know how much that bag cost? It's designer,' Sofia piped up angrily.

'No.'

'Three hundred dollars, and you're going to pay me for it.' Her hands were clenched. It looked like she wanted to punch Shannon.

Shannon looked at us, then looked at her friends.

One of her friends said, 'Maybe it was Tia, Shannon.'

Shannon stared at her. 'Really?'

Chapter Thirty-Four

'Yep; I've seen her talking to Jeff.'

Shannon looked from her friend to us.

'Oh. Sorry.'

'Sofia didn't do it, so leave her alone,' I said.

'Um, yeah,' Shannon said, looking down at her lap.

I turned around and left. Sofia, Tilly and Alisha followed.

'So it *was* Tia! Is she now picking on Sofia?' Tilly asked.

'Yep!' Sofia said. 'And I'm not going to let her tell lies about me!'

The search began for the offender. We circled the school. We spotted her sitting with her group, at a bench near the back oval.

Her back was to us.

'Tia,' I said loudly, trying to grab her attention. She spun to face us. It worked.

We stood glaring down at her. She stared back at us.

'What?' she said. Arrows were in her eyes again. I was the bullseye.

Her group all stopped what they were doing and stared at us.

'You'd better stop making up lies about Sofia, or there'll be trouble,' I stated.

'What? I didn't make up any lies about Sofia. Go jump,' she snapped.

'Oh come on. Shannon just told us,' I retaliated.

The Beast blushed.

'See, caught! Leave us all alone! We will report you Tia. We've got plenty to say,' I said.

She screwed up her face and mimicked my talking. I ignored that. I knew I had hit my mark.

We sauntered back to our spot and examined Sofia's bag. The light brown leather was mottled with dark brown gritty splotches.

'How are you going to get Shannon to pay you for it,' I asked Sofia.

'I'm not. I just said that to see what she'd do. Dad will buy me another one. All's cool,' Sofia said. 'I'll tell him I accidentally dropped it in a puddle. He's always going overseas so he can get me another one. I'm not going to tell him it was Shannon. He'll be up here carrying on if I do. We've dealt with those losers. That's enough for me.'

It felt so good to stand up for myself and my friends.

*

If your friends are in trouble
Get there on the double.
Help them, help them when you can
They will be your greatest fan!

*

Woohoo go Issy! Go Issy! Now let's see if she leaves my group alone.

Chapter Thirty-Five

Wednesday, 24 June

4:18 p.m.

What an awesome friend Sofia is. Guess what she did today? She bought Tilly, Alisha and me a present each, for standing up for her.

It's a charm bracelet. Woohoo! The silver chunky chain she gave me had five charms on it – a heart, star, moon, BFF and my favourite, a pineapple. How cool is that? I'm *so* glad I didn't keep her Pandora bracelet. I'd have felt so guilty now if I had.

I've worn mine all day. ☺

Where mine had a pineapple, Tilly's had a dolphin and Alisha's had an elephant.

I showed my bracelet to Mum.

'Where'd you get that?' she asked me, sounding suspicious.

'My friend Sofia gave it to me.'

'I didn't know you had a friend, Sofia,' Mum said.

Is this going to turn into an interrogation session?

'Sofia and her friend Alisha have been hanging out with Tilly and me at breaks.'

'Oh that's nice,' Mum said. She opened the freezer door and took out some mince. 'So why did she give it to you?'

'She was being bullied and I stood up for her.'

'Oh no, that's awful. You stood up for her?' Mum stared directly at me.

'Yeah, I did.'

'That's nice of you to do that. Just be careful you don't get hurt.' Her eyes narrowed.

'It's all good.' I smiled and waltzed off to my room.

Mum told Dad before I had a chance.

'Princess, I'm proud of you for sticking up for your friend.'

'Thanks Dad.'

I showed him my bracelet.

'Whoa, that must have cost a bit,' he said.

'She's rich, Dad,' I told him, swishing the charms.

Now I'm thinking I should tell Mum and Dad about *me* being bullied. Or could God tell them through a dream or something? ☺

214

Thursday, 16 July

8:08 p.m.

It's been ages since I've written! I've just been so busy. We've had the winter school holidays, and the fam went to Sydney. I loved the animals at Taronga Zoo the best, particularly the giraffes, which I got to feed. I didn't think we'd have enough money to go to Sydney but Dad said it was a treat. He said he got his tax refund back. I also had my cast taken off. ☺ It felt funny when the doctor used his electric saw to cut the plaster. It tickled, and then my arm was all stinky and light. It took a while to get used to having my arm back again. It was really weird.

Straight away Mum gave me the 'you must be careful… it's not fully healed… ra ra ra' speech. I nodded my head like a good daughter and went, 'Yes Mum.'

On the school front, life's been ridiculously good. Tia's backed off and is being amicable, which I'm happy about. The four of us, Tilly, Sofia, Alisha and I continue to hang together at lunchtimes. Sofia and Alisha are lovely. We went to the movies last Saturday. Sofia and Tilly were making silly comments, and I nearly choked on my popcorn, and spat out my Pepsi. I've learnt my lesson. I'm not going to be so possessive of Tilly anymore.

Tim and I have been boarding at the park. He told me he's told Tia to leave me alone which is probably why she's been amicable. They're still going out but I don't think it'll last. He and I are mates and you never know, one day I might be his girlfriend. I'm disappointed that he didn't leave Tia but I can't make him. I still have my mega crush and I still have my piece of notepaper with his name on it under my pillow. ☺

I've kept in contact with Sarah. At the moment she's in Adelaide performing. She sends me messages and keeps encouraging me to be my best. Sarah's amazing and I would love to be like her one day.

I must be acting different as Mum and Dad have both commented on my new attitude. They say I seem happier. I suppose I was pretty sour during the bullying. I still haven't told them. Maybe I should…

Chapter Thirty-Five

Friday, 17 July

4:00 p.m.

I guess things were going too well for me. Something was eventually going to happen. God had to see one more time if I truly had been transformed into a pineapple. Tia became Carla. (I didn't even know Carla's name. It was Alisha who told me.)

At first break today, I was minding my own business, walking to our hangout spot, and I heard 'Bug Eyes'. An electric shock travelled from my head to my toes.

Did I actually hear that?

'Hey, Bug Eyes.'

There it was again. I wasn't hearing things. Someone is making fun of my eyes.

It wasn't Tia. It was a stranger's voice.

I turned towards the words, to see who this new troll was, and I gazed into the screwed up face of a girl I'd never seen before. She was wearing a senior's uniform, and her face had that 'you're going to be my victim if you let me' expression. My heart pounded but I remained calm.

I knew I had two choices. One; I could revert to the old Issy, put my head down and walk away or two, I could be calmly firm and confident.

It would've been much easier to ignore her, and walk away, but I didn't want to have a repeat of the Tia situation. I knew what I had to do.

'Are you talking to me?' I asked her, staring her squarely in the eyeballs.

'Yeah, you.'

'Are you trying to tell me I have big eyes?'

'Yeah, you've got eyes like the nasty bugs I squash.'

'Yeah, I do. I know that.' I remained calm.

She stared at me. Bewilderment was written all over her face. That obviously wasn't what she expected. Ha ha! ☺

Chapter Thirty-Six

You should have seen Carla's face. It was too funny. She looked like she'd been hit in the gob with a mouldy egg.

At that exact moment Tilly appeared by my side.

'Whatsup?' she asked looking from me to Carla.

'Nothin',' Carla said.

'She called me Bug Eyes,' I told Tilly.

'No, I didn't!' Carla's face went red and her voice went high on 'didn't'.

'You're lying. Leave Issy alone!' Tilly told her matter-of-factly.

'Whatever,' Carla said and wandered off.

'You okay?' Tilly asked me.

'Yeah, fine.' I actually felt great!

Tilly grabbed my arm and we skipped off like two little girls.

Tilly told Sofia and Alisha what had happened. Alisha thought she knew who the girl was. We described the girl - our height, plump, freckles, short auburn hair, Senior. Alisha was pretty sure it was Carla. She had the 'bully' reputation.

Instead of sitting there, telling myself what a horrible worthless person I was, I felt fantastic that I'd stood up to her, and I hadn't kept it inside. Even if Tilly hadn't come along, I'd still have told her. I knew Tilly, Sofia and Alisha had my back. If I needed help they would be there for me. ☺

Face your bully, stand up tall.
Face your bully, do not fall.
Tell others, yell it out
Your bully will stop, there's no doubt.

Saturday, 18 July

2:05 p.m.

I received some exciting news today – I got an email from Sarah, asking me if I wanted to be the poster girl for the X-treme Sports Skateboarding Clinic. Duh – YES!

I wondered, why me? I had to email Sarah back and ask her.

'They wanted a tough chick. Well a tough pineapple,' she told me. 'They are trying to get more girls into the sport, and I recommended you.'

I am so stoked. Obviously the X-treme Sports people don't care about my eyes. They were putting ME on a poster that was going to be distributed all around Australia. I WILL BE FAMOUS! ☺ ☺ ☺ So, 'Stick it Tia. Stick it Carla. I will be on a poster, and you won't be!'

I can't stop grinning. Mum and Dad are thrilled and Nathan goes to me, 'Can I take it to school to show everyone?' Oh he's so cute. ☺

Sunday, 19 July

7:30 p.m.

This afternoon I finally spilt the beans about Tia and Carla to Mum and Dad. They were shocked, and Mum had tears in her eyes. She was really upset that I hadn't told her.

I felt bad, that she felt bad. Dad's face was red bull angry. He looked like he was ready to march up to the school, to give them the what for. I had to reassure them both, over and over, that the bullying had stopped, and they didn't need to contact the Principal. They said they wouldn't, on the proviso that I tell them if it started up again. I'm not going to tolerate any more bullying, so I wasn't lying when I said I would.

I'm glad I've told this secret. I let it fly on its invisible paper plane around the Burgess household. ☺ I feel free, like I do when I board.

Chapter Thirty-Seven

Saturday, 25 July

4:13 p.m.

The camera went click, click, click. Who's the most fabulous skateboarding girl at Pinnaroo High? Me, Me, ME! ☺ It was so much fun having my photo taken for the promo posters. The photographer took snaps of me holding my board, and doing some basic tricks. It was like being a Hollywood celebrity. I really could get used to this. When they're printed, I'm going to stick the posters all over my bedroom wall. ☺

Lights, Camera, Action, Pose
That's how the story goes
Poster girl for X-treme boarding sports
Cruising and tricking on the basketball courts.

9:15 p.m.

You know it's amazing. I feel like I'm a different person. The Issy I was in March, is now in July, a new creation. Tonight I've been thinking about the things that have changed and these are what I've come up with:

Sarah's pineapple strategy has helped me to cope with my anxiety. I still get some of my symptoms but I know I can work through them, and face my fears. I'm sweet, strong, courageous and spiky. And sometimes I even wear a sparkly crown. ☺

I'm believing in myself and my abilities.

I'm learning to look at things positively, not negatively.

I know that if things do go wrong, it's all right. I just need to pick myself back up and keep on trying.

I CAN stand up for myself and if the problem is too big, I just need to tell my friends (and parents or teachers if need be) who will protect and help me.

I realise that the people who matter don't care that I have big eyes. In reality it's only been two kids out of the whole school who've been mean to me. I need to care less about those two (or anyone else who teases me), and more about my friends and adults, like Sarah and Miss O'Keefe, who accept me for who I am. (Sofia even told me that I'm an inspiration to her which blew me away.)

I know skateboarding is my talent which I will continue to work on. Mum's ordered a face helmet – like a Gridiron helmet. I'm going to be trying more difficult tricks so I'm going to need it.

And finally, the fact that I don't have the boyfriend I want, is fine too. It's nice just being friends with him. In the future things may change. ☺

Life's good in the world of Issy Burgess!

5:07 p.m.

Dad came home this afternoon with a love gift for me. That's a present for no special occasion. I looked at the plain white thick plastic bag, wondering what was in it.

I peeked inside. There was a box but the end of it was black, not giving away any clues. I took the gift out and stared at the picture on the front of the box. I let out a loud squeal and lunged at Dad, kissing his cheek. Jumping up and down, I opened the box and pulled out the item.

It was a skateboard with orange and green pineapples printed all over it.

'I LOVE it Dad! Thank you so much.' I cuddled the board to my chest.

Dad grinned at me.

'Cool!' Nathan said.

'Dad, you're the best!' I said, kissing him on his cheek.

Dad blushed. 'Glad you like it Princess.'

I carried my new board back to my room. I moved my longboard from the top shelf of my shoe stand, and put it on the second shelf, rearranging the other shelves. My pineapple board now took pride of place.

I Skyped Tilly, Alisha and Sofia, for a four-way chat. I had to show it to them. ☺

Sunday, 26 July

2:18 p.m.

I'm off to the skate park to try out my new board. I can't wait. Woohoo!

Ride high Pineapple! ☺

About the Story

In Ride High Pineapple, Issy has a craniofacial syndrome called Crouzon syndrome. It is a rare syndrome that affects both boys and girls, and occurs all over the world. The gene affected makes the bones of the skull and face stop growing too soon. Basically the bones are small so the head is misshapen, the eyes are bulgy and the face is flat. Depending on the severity, the child may need no operations or many. The syndrome does not affect intelligence or the person's ability to have a good life.

Myself and two of my children have this syndrome.

Here are two links if you would like to know more about Crouzon syndrome:
www.youtube.com/watch?v=RCcvVzrstBM
www.ccakids.com/crouzon-syndrome.html

Or you can find me and others at:
www.facebook.com/International-Crouzon-Syndrome-Support-Group-146204398727264/

In the story Issy also suffers from severe anxiety and bullying. If you feel like Issy, you need to talk to someone so they can help you to cope. If you can't talk to an adult at home or school or youth group, you can contact Kids Helpline, Headspace (for teens), or Beyondblue in Australia.

Kids Helpline - https://kidshelpline.com.au/

Headspace - http://headspace.org.au/

Beyondblue - https://www.beyondblue.org.au/

At the hospital, Issy has a visit from Captain Starlight. Captain Starlight is one of the ways that the Starlight Children's Foundation helps sick children. Their mission is 'To brighten the lives of seriously ill children and their families'. You can find out more at - https://starlight.org.au/

Acknowledgements

My heartfelt thanks go to:

- My wonderful husband Joe, and my beautiful children Melissa, Nick and Jessica, who love and support me, with everything I do.
- My parents, Viv and Beryl Collins, who loved me and helped me to face the world growing up. I am who I am because they believed in me.
- God for His love and putting this story in my heart.
- Helen Low, who took me under her wing in 2014 and encouraged me to write this story. Though the finished version is quite different to the original, if it wasn't for Helen, I may never have finished the first manuscript.
- My writer friends, particularly Jacqui Halpin, Alison Stegert, Raelene Purtill, Karen Tyrrell, Charmaine Clancy, June Perkins and Melanie Little, for their advice and critiquing along the way.
- Deb McNair and Sally Odgers who edited my story and helped me to make it the best story it could be.
- Anthony Puttee from Book Cover Café for helping me publish the book.

- My friends in the International Crouzon Syndrome Support Group, and the Australian Crouzon and Pfeiffer Support Group who I share my life journey with.
- The Children's Craniofacial Association and Monica Mossholder in the USA who read my manuscript and believed in my story. I am so humbled by their endorsement.
- My friends, old and new, who have been with me through the ups and downs of my life.

About the Author

Jenny Woolsey is a writer, blogger, teacher and advocate for people with facial differences, mental illness and disabilities. She has a Diploma of Teaching (Primary), Bachelor of Education, Master of Education (Honours), and a Certificate in Creative Writing. Because she loves helping children, in 2016 she is studying a Certificate IV in Youth Work.

Home is in the north of Brisbane, in Queensland, Australia, with her husband, three magnificent children, three spirited cats and her cute fluffy dog.

Jenny started writing stories when she was little. As a teenager, poetry was her favourite genre. In 2014 Jenny decided it was time to begin writing Ride High Pineapple. The subject matter in Ride High Pineapple being close to her heart, as Jenny and two of her children have Issy's craniofacial syndrome. Anxiety and depression also live in the Woolsey household.

Jenny writes to help children and teens who feel different, shy, anxious, or don't fit in. She understands as she was all of those growing up!

You are good enough – in fact you are more than that –
you are perfect just the way you are!
Remember, no matter what you look like or feel like,
you are valuable and can achieve great things in life!
It's okay to be different!

Jenny ☺

You can find Jenny in many places:

Email: jenny.woolsey@hotmail.com
Website: http://jennywoolsey.com/
Blog: Jenny Woolsey – The ABCs of Life:

http://jennywoolsey.blogspot.com.au/
Blog: Crouzons, Downs and Me....Love and Life:
http://crouzonsdownsandme.blogspot.com.au/
Facebook:- www.facebook.com/JennyWoolsey8/
Twitter: @Jenny_Woolsey
YouTube: www.youtube.com/user/jennyw67

Coming 2016... Brockwell the Brave

Twelve year old Viking, Brockwell Ness, lives on a dragon farm in the village of Enga. He would prefer to be at the healing hut than at home with the scary juvenile and adult dragons or around the village where Colden picks on him. When Brockwell's father doesn't come back from a mission to capture an injured dragon, he has to make a decision. Will Brockwell be able to face his giants?

http://jennywoolsey.com/

CPSIA information can be obtained
at www.ICGtesting.com
Printed in the USA
BVHW080726290721
613100BV00003B/520